Angels on the Bridge

A Novel

Matt Kozar

Little Gerry Publishing

For Doug

CONTENTS

ACKNOWLEDGMENTS

Writing is a solitary art, but the unwavering support of mentors, friends and family fueled my drive to complete this book. A special thanks to journalist, author and copy editor David Stout. Kristen Young provided additional editing guidance. The talented Joseph Kindya used his pencil and brush to create a beautiful illustration that is the book's cover. Lauren Harris assisted with the cover design and layout. To all of my teachers, from elementary school to graduate school and beyond, thank you for showing me the art of storytelling. Lastly, and most importantly, my parents, Kathy and Russ Kozar, deserve a standing ovation for encouraging me to never stop dreaming.

CHAPTER 1
THE OLD STONE BRIDGE

James was dismissive of the stars. The pinpricks of light felt out of reach. All he knew about them was what he'd read in books — twinkling balls of gas.

He preferred something more tangible like wood — maple, elm, mahogany, ash — something he could shape into a desk or a table. He'd built Lily a bookcase in the carpenter's shop where he apprenticed. She'd filled the shelves with nursing textbooks and set aside one row for Shakespeare; *Julius Caesar* was her favorite play. Still, he found himself drawn to the night sky and gazed at the heavens through the skylights of the bar. His shift was almost over.

On this night, a stream of sweat snaked a path down his forehead and dripped into his kind eyes. The glowing sphere above became a blurry mass. He abandoned constellation hunting and retreated to the metal sink to wash away the burning. The knobs felt cold in the darkness, but when he turned them, scalding water blasted against the basin and splashed his white T-shirt, jeans and black-canvas sneakers. Hot water seeped into his clothes and burned his skin. He adjusted the faucets as fast as he could and leaned in for a rinse, unaware of the open, overhead cabinet — one that he'd built.

He cracked his skull against the sharp edge. Beer mugs stacked atop one another toppled over and nearly delivered a second blow to his head. A large stein smashed into a thousand pieces on the stone-tiled floor.

The 23-year-old cried out in pain. Blood squirted from a gash above his right eye and streamed down his cheek. It mixed with sweat and seeped into his mouth — tasted like salty metal. The water from the faucet washed away the sanguine mix, which twirled down the drain. His head felt as if it'd been split open with a wooden nightstick. His grandfather kept one hidden underneath the bed. "For protection," he'd say. "You never know what might come through the front door!"

The bloodied bartender brushed back his dirty-blond hair and compressed his wound with a white towel, the same one he'd used to wipe down the bar. It smelled of stale beer and whiskey.

"Are you all right?" asked a petite waitress who disguised a sliver of amusement with a furled brow. Despite her best efforts, she couldn't suppress the smirk and pressed her delicate fingers to her rosy lips to force away the smile. "What have you done this time?"

"I'm fine," he shot back. The towel covering his face muffled his voice. "I'm... just... fine."

He blushed, and his face turned tomato-red. His

pride was more bruised than his forehead.

"You might be the clumsiest person in the entire world, but for some strange reason, I still love you."

Lily giggled and the tiny hairs on James's arms stood tall. Her sugary chuckle tickled every nerve in his body. It was, quite simply, the most mellifluous sound he'd ever heard.

The heels of Lily's cowboy boots clicked and clacked against the bar floor, stained by decades of spilled liquor, beer and tobacco ash. Her golden-blond hair bounced as she glided around the room. Jeans ripped at the knees. Denim sleeves rolled up to her elbows. Dimples on both cheeks punctuated an ear-to-ear smile. Sincere blue eyes invited the world into her warm domain. It's what he loved the most about her.

"Here's a fresh towel that doesn't smell like booze," she said and draped the warm compress across James's forehead before peeling it back to inspect the swollen cut.

Lily dipped a second towel in a shot glass filled with vodka and dabbed the gash.

"This might sting a bit, so hold still."

James screamed and kicked his feet into the air.

"A bit!" he protested. "That really hurt!"

"Do you want it to get infected or not?"

Her gentle fingers brushed his cheek, and he felt the cold metal of the ruby ring he'd given her as a birthday present — not an engagement ring but a promise of one to come, whenever he could muster up enough cash.

Quiet Saturday nights at The Dragon's Den weren't helping to build his savings. The bar was dead and that meant another evening without tips.

3

It'd been that way for several weekends in a row. College was in summer recess, and the crowds were sparse. It wasn't ideal, but as long as she was by his side, that was all that mattered.

"You're a woman of many talents," he said from underneath the wet towel. "Nurse by day. Bartender by night. Not only do you serve drinks, but you also care for the wounded drunks after the brawl."

"I love you even when you act like a fool," Lily said. She stood on her toes to reach his neck and kissed him below his ear. "You're lucky it's only the two of us tonight because otherwise the entire bar would be laughing at you."

When James and his older brother were growing up, their mother told them they'd *know* the moment they met their soulmates. "It's like finding your other half," she'd say. "Two puzzle pieces coming together."

James was incredulous to the idea of one-true love. He had many girlfriends over the years, and all of the relationships were *fine* — how he described them to his brother Will — until they ended for one reason or another. He figured that was the way things were supposed to go — make it work until it doesn't. Maybe it was a matter of finding the best one, not necessarily the one. He branded his thinking a pragmatic approach to love.

Then, he met Lily.

The moment remained etched in his memory, even the date and time — January 1st at 1:11 a.m.

James caught a glimpse of the repeating sequence on the crooked clock hanging from a rusty nail in the wall of The Dragon's Den and thought it a good omen. The bar had been packed that night for New

Year's Eve. As he and his college buddies saluted their last semester of school with liquor, he watched a tiny waitress drift from table to table like a graceful dancer. Her turquoise floral dress fluttered with elegance. Bronze skin. Eyes that sparkled in the dim light. He prayed she'd look his way, but his rowdy friends blocked his line of sight.

"Another round," his classmate Ernie shouted, slurring nearly every consonant. He wobbled as he turned to face James. "I like living in a town named after a writer. Makes me feel... *smart*! I just hate (hiccup) that the weather (another hiccup) is too damn *cold*!"

Ernie nearly fell over before regaining his balance. A redhead, nicknamed Ginger, slid one arm around James's shoulders and the other on their inebriated friend.

"I hear the best way to stay warm on a cold night is to drink whiskey," Ginger said. "I bet that's what Emerson did when he lived here in New York."

James rolled his eyes.

"Emerson lived in Massachusetts, you idiot, and studied at Harvard. Aren't you a lit major?"

"Shut up — let's drink!"

The trio clicked their glasses before gulping down the cheap whiskey. The alcohol burned a path down their throats and into their bellies. Each made a bitter face.

"That'll put hair on a man's chest," the redhead said.

"Do you even plan to go to class this semester?"

"I don't know. My goal is to study as little as possible and see if I can get away with it. A few books here. A few papers there. I think that's doable, and dare I say, commendable."

"Cheers (hiccup) to that," Ernie said.

But before James could lift the glass for another sip, Lily reappeared. This time, she was writing down a customer's order. When she looked up from her notes, she locked eyes with James, and his heart melted on the spot. He knew at that moment, everything his mother had said was true. It'd been two years since that night, and his feelings remained just as strong.

"Does your head still hurt?" she asked.

Lily replaced the wet towel with a plastic bag filled with ice cubes. James jumped back from the shock of the cold to his skin.

"Better... freezing... but better."

He titled his head backward and spotted the fuzzy, celestial orb that had dominated his attention prior to injuring himself. Stars surrounded the moon in a sea of darkness.

His eyes still burned, and he couldn't trust them. "Full moon?"

"Looks like it, so be careful out there."

She brushed his hair with her hand and pecked his cheek with her lips.

"I have a favor to ask," Lily said. "Would you be okay if I left early? I've got a mid-term tomorrow and haven't studied. I can't wait to be done with all of these exams — only one more semester to go!"

"I'll close up shop and meet you back at home. Don't worry about me."

"But I do worry about you. Promise not to impale yourself on kitchen knives? I won't be here to rescue you."

"Comedy is not your strong suit, so stick to

nursing and bartending."

Lily pressed two of her fingers to his lips to keep them closed and kissed the ends of her fingertips resting on his mouth.

"When are you going to take me to the beach? You know it's my favorite place," she said. "We could go to Florida, or even (she winked) Hawaii!"

"One day soon, but in the meantime, you'll have to settle for something less exotic like the lake."

James thought nursing a fitting profession for Lily. Helping others was in her DNA. If she spotted someone struggling to cross the street or carry groceries, she'd be the first to rush over and assist.

James's buddies left Emerson following graduation — Ginger was studying law, and Ernie took over the family farm — but he chose to stay with Lily. Bartending paid the bills, yet carpentry was his true passion. During the day, he apprenticed at a woodworking shop and learned how to build furniture. He dreamed of one day building a home where he and Lily could start a family.

"I love you," he said.

She kissed him one last time.

"I love you too."

"Goodbye, my darling."

*

James's tattoo came alive in the silvery moonlight shining into the bar. His rolled-up sleeves revealed an armed crusader on horseback etched in grayish-blue ink that stretched from the top of his skinny arm near his shoulder down to the middle of his bicep. The knight's cape fluttered while he rode a muscular horse wearing a yellow caparison — one hand on the reins and the other grasping a spear topped with a crucifix. He planted the point of his weapon into the mouth of a prostrated dragon that cried out in agony. The beast withered as death neared. Its claws stretched outward in one last-feeble attempt to defend itself.

James's friends teased that the sword-fighting body art contrasted with his true personality, but he disagreed. As a thoughtful craftsman who spent hours carving intricate details into wood, James appreciated the skill set of the tattoo artist and how one tiny needle filled with ink could create something beautiful.

He'd gotten the permanent mark of the venerated saint because of his namesake — James St. George. He also loved the inspiring legend surrounding the martyr. One version held that St. George was a Roman soldier executed by the emperor for not recanting his Christian faith. The other account was that he'd slain a dragon threatening a town's drinking water, and subsequently, rescued a princess who'd been offered to the dragon as a sacrifice. After St. George defeated the beast, the townspeople converted to Christianity.

James scrubbed the beer mugs. Steam from the hot water warmed his face, and he wiped away sweat collecting along his brow. No need to be blinded again and repeat what happened earlier; his head still throbbed.

The bar's quietness was a sharp contrast to most nights when the boisterous regulars caused a ruckus. James knew them all: the neighborhood drunks in search of their daily fix; the prowling divorcees on the hunt for companionship, if only for a night; and college kids satisfied with cut-rate beer that tasted like piss and cheap vodka that doubled as turpentine. He wondered how their young stomachs could handle the excess alcohol.

The stories were plentiful. There was the time his former mathematics professor, Dr. Christof Weber, walked into the bar wearing a blond wig, a red wrap dress, stiletto heels, eyeshadow, blush and lipstick. But the professor hadn't bothered to disguise his voice and drop his German accent, so when he said, "I will have a vodka cranberry," James, who was looking down at the cash register, replied "Of course, professor." He jumped two feet in the air when he saw the mathematician decked out in women's apparel. Weber would have made a pretty woman, if not for the hairy hands.

On another night, Ernie's jealous ex-girlfriend tracked him to his usual spot at the corner table, where he was on a date with an attractive brunette. The frying-pan attack — as it would be called for years to come — was vicious and without warning. She said nothing as she swung the metal weapon at the back of his head. He passed out and face-planted into a pile of poutine.

But no theatrics on this night. The weary-eyed bartender put the last of the plates on the drying rack, wiped down the metallic ledge where the cooks left food for the servers, tucked the stools and chairs underneath the tables and mopped the stone floor. He sighed with relief and chugged what was left of his lukewarm beer.

Little Gerry was fast asleep in his terrarium. The three-foot long ball python was curled in-between a rock and a log. The snake awoke long enough to gaze up at the bartender refilling his water bowl before resting his head back on the mulch scattering the glass enclosure. James thought Little Gerry was a handsome snake — if snakes were ever handsome. He was dark brown with blotchy-light brown spots, and despite his fearsome expression and beady eyes, he was shy. Drunken college students would stare into the makeshift habitat to catch a glimpse of the bar's mascot, but Little Gerry wanted none of it. He'd slither away from the prying eyes and hide underneath a plant. Sometimes, James wrapped Little Gerry around his neck and served drinks, which amused customers. They'd point and laugh at the dumbfounded reptile. James found it curious that the expressionless snake could bring so much happiness.

His brother had given him Little Gerry as a 16th birthday present, mostly as a joke. "What am I going to do with this thing?" James said to Will. At the time, Little Gerry was only 5 inches long, hence his nickname. But the snake got bigger and James grew fonder of his unusual pet. He recognized that snakes had reputations as vicious, cold-blooded hunters with razor-sharp fangs — not to mention that Garden of Eden thing. Still, James thought the characterizations were unfair. Little Gerry was different. Once, he escaped from his glass tank and went missing for two weeks. When James heard his mother screaming in the laundry room, he knew Little Gerry had reappeared. The ball python was curled-up underneath warm laundry that had just come from the drier.

"He looks like he's smiling," James said.

"Get him away from me now!" his mother screamed.

He'd lifted the happy snake in his hands and carried him back to his enclosure.

James loved Little Gerry and decided it was selfish not to share him with others. So, he got permission from the owner of The Dragon's Den to setup a terrarium in the middle of the bar. Little Gerry became a hit overnight. Toasting the snake was an evening ritual. The reptile would stare blankly through the glass as dozens lifted their drinks in his honor. "I'm jealous because he's more popular than me," James told Lily.

Little Gerry appeared to be resting well underneath his heat lamp. James brushed his fingers across the snake's scales.

"Good night, buddy. Time for me to go."

The Dragon's Den sat on a promenade along the sleepy Willow River that flowed underneath what folks in town called the old stone bridge. The century-old structure looked out of place among the gas stations, chain restaurants, car dealerships and boutique shops that made Emerson like every other American town. Locals joked they'd sometimes see trolls emerge from the bridge's damp underbelly to collect tolls. In reality, they were can collectors and vagabonds harassing drivers for spare change. The bridge was a link from one world to another. All of the land east of the cobblestone roadway led to lush-dense forest and a vast countryside replete with bucolic cottages and farms. West of the bridge included the town square, the college and businesses.

Old River Way was the main artery in and out of Emerson. Cars, delivery trucks and taxis used it to get across the bridge to the center of town. But tonight was different. No cars. No vagabond-like trolls. Only the cacophony of cicadas clicking in the night.

James hiked along a paved path that stretched underneath the bridge's archway and up a steep hill toward the street. Iron lampposts provided just enough of a dim-orangey glow for him to find the stone steps. He swatted mosquitoes attempting to land on his arms and neck. His T-shirt, wet and heavy from sweat, clung to his body. James squeezed his stinging eyes shut and wiped away a pool of perspiration. When he felt confident his eyeballs were safe from more burning, he opened them wide, only to be startled by a zigzagging light.

The dancing firefly left intermittent trails of yellow in the darkness that smelled of honeysuckle. The solitary bug was four-sizes larger than the average firefly, which explained why its glow was almost as bright as the street lamp. The insect cut through the humidity and shadowed James on his trek to the bridge. Every so often, it rested on his shoulder before taking flight to lead the way.

"Coming home with me, buddy?" he whispered to his new friend. "I hope you're as fast as my pickup."

James appreciated the companionship on his lonely walk, and a bit of extra light couldn't hurt, even if it came from a superbug on steroids. Plus, the firefly was keeping the pesky mosquitoes away.

He reached street level and the base of the old stone bridge. His footsteps echoed on the stone slabs and became part of the symphony of the night. Whistling wind. Bustling leaves. Chirping crickets. His quiet march through the darkness felt different from his afternoon stroll to work, when people packed the park benches lining the water. An elderly woman positioned in the same spot every day would dip her brush in water colors and make gentle strokes on a canvas; she painted the bridge in every season. Even The Dragon's Den came alive when the regulars slipped in for a liquid lunch before shuffling back to the doldrums of their jobs.

The roar of a car engine interrupted the stillness and spooked the firefly. The insect jumped off James's shoulder and shot up like a helicopter. Its burning yellow hue faded as it flew toward the stars. James had never seen any insect fly in a straight-vertical line. He scoured the sky for a trace of the disappearing bug but lost track of it. In its place, he spotted millions of stars in unusual patterns. He used his finger to trace out a constellation in the shape of a bear.

The mechanical growling returned and broke his concentration. The drag racer revved his engine before shifting gears. The tires screeched and seared black rubber streaks into the asphalt. The car spun in circles and made donuts on the pavement. Gray smoke climbed toward the moon. The fire engine-red coupe crisscrossed the avenues and blew through stop signs. James whipped his head back toward town for a glimpse of the rocket shooting down empty streets and into the shadows. Flame decals swallowed its front grill.

James shook his head in disgust and continued walking toward his truck. He ignored the noise and forced his thoughts to return to Lily and her perfume — sweet amber with a hint of sandalwood. It'd been less than an hour since she'd left the bar, but he missed her already.

"Parting is such sweet sorrow that I shall say

goodnight till it be morrow."

It was the only line from *Romeo and Juliet* that he remembered. James had needed to fulfill an English requirement, so Lily made him take her literature course — "The Musings of a Master." At the time, it seemed like a good idea, but he didn't anticipate the advanced-reading requirements and subsequent essay assignments. He also failed to appreciate Shakespeare's couplets and iambic pentameter.

"It's such a complicated way to tell a simple story," he'd say.

Lily wrote most of his papers — she was the better writer anyway — but he did enjoy that famous line, mostly because it was her favorite.

He thought about the engagement ring he wanted to buy, and the money he'd been saving. It wasn't much, but it could be enough to buy a decent stone if he negotiated. His cousin had recommended a diamond dealer in Manhattan. James planned to take the train south to New York City one weekend when Lily was studying. Waiting was no longer an option. It was time to propose.

Again — the rumbling returned. The distinctive roar got louder. His shoelaces came into view as the stones got brighter. Blinding all-encompassing white light enveloped his body. A deafening hum drowned out all other noise. The smell of burnt rubber mixed with sweet jasmine.

And then… silence.

CHAPTER 2
REFLECTIONLESS

James forced open his heavy eyelids and felt as if he'd awoken from a nap that'd lasted years. Streaks of blues and reds zigzagged before him at lightning speed. The world was blurry and quiet; he couldn't even hear his own breathing. The overbearing odor of gasoline burned his nostrils and filtered up into his head. He keeled over and grabbed his belly. He thought he'd either throw up or pass out.

The spinning slowed just enough for figures to take shape. James watched half-a-dozen men dressed in navy-blue huddling around a person on the ground. They lifted the half-naked body covered in cuts, scrapes and bruises onto a slender red board and strapped an oxygen mask to the victim's face, but it didn't appear to help. His chest wasn't moving. Bare feet dangled off the edge of the board. Tattered jeans fluttered in the wind. The men in blue transferred the victim to a metal gurney, which they hoisted into an ambulance.

"One hell of a crash, dude," said a lanky teen with twiggy arms.

If it hadn't been for the stranger speaking to him, James would've thought he'd gone deaf. The high-pitched crackly voice — somewhere between a boy's and a man's — was the only thing he could hear. It was as if he and the teenager were stuck in a glass cube and were casual observers to a world in motion.

James tried to maneuver off the cold stone but struggled to stand. His legs betrayed him, and he stumbled but was saved by the bridge's edge, which prevented him from tumbling into the river.

"I don't know what happened." James' head was still spinning. "I was walking to my truck… there was a firefly following me… bigger than any firefly I'd ever seen… then a noise… maybe a car… then… I can't remember."

"No worries, man." The teen patted James on the shoulder. "Don't beat yourself up over it."

The young man was dressed more for Southern California than upstate New York. His board shorts had a magenta-floral pattern that complemented purple flip-flops. A sleeveless T-shirt showcased slender, olive-colored arms that lead to hands large enough to palm a basketball. A small patch of stubble on his chin matched the bleached-blond hair poking out from underneath a backward-baseball cap with a sewn patch of a surfboard on the front. The teen was at least 6 feet tall, and his awkward limbs threw everything out of proportion.

"Can you tell me what happened?" James asked. He felt more stable on his feet and stood upright without any help from the wall.

"Dude, that car was going super-fast and lost

control. The crash was so loud."

"I remember a red car speeding through the streets."

"That was the one that crashed — right over there." The teen pointed to a wreck 50 feet away. "That thing was all over the place!"

The muscle car was perched on the edge of the stone bridge and suspended at a precarious angle. Its front tires were on the road, but its undercarriage rested atop the sidewall. The back tires dangled above the water. One strong gust of wind and the heap of metal would fall into the muddy river. The mangled mess was unrecognizable. Its engine block was crushed — both ends were smashed in and all of its inner workings exposed. A bent lamppost lay across the crumpled hood. Dirt and plants covered the cracked windshield; the driver had hit several planters filled with shrubs and hydrangeas along the path of destruction. All of the airbags had deployed, but no one was inside.

"Did you see the impact?" James asked his new friend.

"Unfortunately, I did. Wicked crash! The car smashed into the old stone bridge like nothing I've ever seen."

James cocked his head and stared up at the stranger.

"Why can't I hear anything other than your voice?"
"Oh, right!"

The teen snapped his fingers, and the world around them came alive with sound, as if the walls of their glass cube had disappeared. Ambulance sirens blared. The chattering of the first responders competed against their emergency radios. A tow

truck beeped and reversed up the bridge, inching
closer to the wrecked sports car. The Willow River
rippled under the bridge.

"How'd you do that?"

The teen ignored James's question and turned
toward three police officers flanking a muscular man
with brown-hair and hazel eyes. He was wearing a
black short-sleeved collared shirt, khakis and untied
boat shoes. He tripped over his laces and stumbled
forward. A burly officer stretched out his arm to
catch the man, who subsequently smacked away the
cop's helping hand.

"Don't... touch me... you bastard," he shouted.
"You don't... do you know... why don't you go... do
you know who I am?"

The phalanx of officers grew larger as the driver
got louder.

"I asked... do you... know?" the man repeated
with a hiccup. "I'm the... designated... driver."

The cops stood in a protective stance and
surrounded the drunk, whose bloodshot eyes popped
out in a ferocious rage.

"My poor car! Look... at my... car! All I did...
was... pass... cab!"

"Sir, we need you to come with us," a sergeant
demanded.

He approached the driver who shoved the cop in
the chest. Before he could strike again, two patrol
officers tackled and handcuffed the man, who
squirmed on the ground like a worm and drunkenly
screamed, "I'm suing! I'm a private citizen!"

The police carried his twisting body into the back
of a cruiser, where he disappeared behind the glaring
red and blue lights. His ranting became distant

background noise.

"My friends call me Chuck," the teen said.

He stuck out his oversized hand for a shake. James grabbed it and felt a spark of electricity shoot up his right arm and into his shoulder and chest before fizzling somewhere in his belly. The hairs on his neck stood straight up. It felt like the time he shoved the prong of father's belt buckle into an electrical outlet when he was child; the shock had paralyzed his body, and he was too afraid to even cry. James arched his eyebrows at the teen, who smiled back.

"My name is James."

"Cool dude. I'm gonna' call you Jimmy," Chuck said, indifferent as to whether James approved of his new nickname. "Come this way, so I can show you something."

The two walked toward the bright, flashing lights of the ambulance, which had since turned off its sirens. James shielded his eyes, still sensitive from the burst of white light he'd experienced a few minutes earlier. The paramedics were chatting with a group of officers next to the smashed car but none seemed to be in any hurry. Chuck opened the doors to the back of the ambulance and jumped inside.

"Hey, don't do that," James shouted.

"Chill out Jimmy. Trust me and hop in."

James shook his head, looked around to see if anyone was watching and reluctantly followed Chuck into the ambulance, shutting the doors behind them. The man covered in blood on the stretcher wasn't breathing, and James now understood why the paramedics had no intention of taking him to the hospital; his next stop would be the medical

examiner's office. Grit, sweat and gravel matted
down the man's hair. A broken femur protruded
from underneath his torn pants. A deep abrasion
stretched across his naked chest. He looked young,
but it was hard to discern an exact age because the
oxygen mask covered his face.

"Is he dead?" James asked.

Chuck nodded. "I'm afraid so. I'll take off his
mask for you to see."

"Don't do that! We shouldn't be back…"

James froze.

A droning sound filled his head. The face on the
gurney. It was impossible. There was no way it could
be his own, and how could it be if he was standing
and talking and breathing and moving. Plus, he was
only 23 years old — too young to die.

Images flashed before his eyes at lightning speed
much like the kaleidoscope he played with as a boy,
but instead of scenes from the past, he saw memories
yet to happen: the phone call to his mother about his
next visit home; the candlelight dinner on the beach
where he planned to propose to Lily; the honeymoon
to the topical island; the birth of his three children;
the convertible ride on an autumn day; the ice-cream
birthday cakes; the rocking chair on the front porch.
A life replete with love.

James St. George died at 1:00 a.m. on a humid
Saturday in July.

*

It wasn't the way he wanted to go. No chance to
defend himself or react. His body was exposed,
battered, beaten and broken in the back of a sterile

ambulance. James clutched his own clammy hand hanging off the gurney. If only he could somehow jolt himself back to life. He'd read stories about people who had near-death experiences — pronounced dead on the operating room table only to come alive on the way to the morgue.

"Sorry, but there's nothing you can do," Chuck said, as if he'd been reading James's thoughts. He patted him on the back again. "It was your time. Part of your journey."

But James had no interest in hearing about a journey. He'd expected death would come for him one day when he was a wrinkled ball with a few teeth, some strands of gray hair and a handful of memories rolling around in a slowing mind. But that was far away, or at least he thought it was.

"I don't understand," he said with desperation in his voice. "I thought I had more time. I thought I had a lot more time. There's so much I have to do."

His voice trailed off, and his glassy eyes swelled with tears that cascaded down his cheeks. Each droplet left a shiny trail on his skin before splashing onto the ambulance's rubber-floor mat. He buried his head in his hands. The sorrow penetrated his core and engendered a loneliness he'd never experienced. He realized that he'd never see any of them ever again. Lily, his parents and brother were now faded memories to be stored away like photos in an album. He already missed their faces, smells and voices.

Melancholy filled the ambulance. James looked at Chuck, who was also crying. The two experienced the same emotions because they shared an etheric bond that had been in place long before the crash.

"You'll see them again," Chuck said. "I promise.

They're not gone forever — only for right now. It's just that you've got to go a separate way."

James ignored his new companion, brushed aside his arm and fled the ambulance.

The stars focused their beams of light on the old stone bridge. The firefighters, police and paramedics didn't notice James walking underneath the yellow crime scene tape and running past the crumpled debris and toppled planters. He leaned over the stone wall and stared into the river but saw no reflection. Instead, he watched a school of glimmering fish dance near the water's surface, brought to life by the moonlight.

Chuck whispered into James's ear, "It's time to go."

CHAPTER 3
FISHING IN THE RIVER

A cobalt sky poked through the black canvas, and the pulsating stars dimmed until they disappeared. The moon gave way to a sunset that sent streaks of radiant oranges and reds bursting over a snow-capped mountain range.

The mangled car, the stench of spilled fuel, the ambulance sirens and the white flashes from the crash investigator's camera were gone, replaced by chirping sparrows, wheat fields that swayed with the breeze and a river teeming with fish. A rainbow of colors flowed downstream with the current.

James sucked in the piney air and let it flow through his body. He absorbed all of the sights and sounds of this new, yet familiar place — he'd been here before but couldn't remember when. His clothes were the same as they were on the old stone bridge: white T-shirt; worn jeans; black canvas sneakers. He rolled up his sleeve and checked his arm — the tattoo of St. George was still there.

"I've been waiting for you," said an elderly man standing on a rock in the middle of the river. His gray hair was parted to one side, and his wrinkly skin showed his age like a tree trunk with innumerable rings. The man beckoned with his left hand, while holding a fishing rod in his right. An opened tackle box revealed a collection of feathery lures.

"Come closer and take a look," he said.

The fishing pole jerked back and forth as the old man battled a trout, the largest James had ever seen. The fisherman balanced atop a flat stone, and his ability in no way mirrored his timeworn appearance. He moved with the agility of a man half his age and yanked the rod to gain the upper hand, but the trout was not giving up. It nearly pulled the old man off the slippery rock as it swam for its life. Somehow, he held his footing all while reeling in the line a few inches at a time.

"Is that you, Grandpa?

"Good to see you again, my boy!"

Grandpa's booming voice thundered across the valley. He grabbed the brim of his canvas hat and tipped it forward toward James.

"You've grown quite a bit since I last saw you. Back then, you were just a few feet tall. Of course, I've been…"

He stopped midsentence as the fish made one last attempt at a getaway and pulled hard to the right.

"Not this time! Almost… there…c'mon… GOT HIM!"

The trout danced on the end of Grandpa's line. Its reddish, shiny scales shimmered in the sun's rays.

"What a beauty! I'd bet maybe 50 pounds. Biggest one I've ever caught in these waters!"

"It's beautiful," James said. "Will you keep it?"

"Well, let's take a closer look."

But as Grandpa lifted his wooden rod to inspect the prize catch, the pole splintered and broke in half, and the lucky trout splashed into the river. Ripples pulsated from the spot where the fish made its great escape, disappearing into the underwater rainbow.

"Can you believe it!" Grandpa shouted, undeterred by his misfortune. His mouth curled into a smile, and he bellowed into hearty laughter. "Some days you get the fish, and other days the fish gets you."

The old man hopped from rock to rock like a playful child until he reached the grassy riverbank where he bear-hugged James.

"I've missed you so much," Grandpa said and kissed his grandson on both cheeks. "I've been waiting for you. I know you've been through a lot. That crash was something awful." He stared deep into James's eyes and lowered his voice. "Are you okay?"

James broke from Grandpa's gaze and looked away.

"To be honest... I don't know. It all happened so fast. Where am I?"

"You've been through quite a shock, and it will take time, but I promise it will all make sense."

Grandpa's look of concern morphed into his famous grin.

"To answer your question, you're in heaven. To be more specific, you're in my heaven. Pretty nice, isn't it? You probably don't remember me taking you fishing when you were young, but we'd go every summer weekend to the reservoir."

James remembered those warm evenings on the

rowboat near the lake house. Grandpa would pack a cooler filled with sodas, sandwiches and snacks and would buy worms from the bait-and-tackle shop. They'd catch everything from striped bass to pickerel to herring and pike but would never keep the fish. Grandpa would always unhook the lures from their gaping mouths and toss the creatures back into the water. He said he never liked to see anything suffer, and neither did James.

"Those were the happiest days of my life," Grandpa said. "Seeing your eyes widen when you caught a trout filled me with joy. My fishing prodigy was following in my footsteps. You loved nature as much I did. We'd fish for hours and race home for dinner or risk the wrath of grandma."

"Is she here too?"

"Oh — she's here. I gather she's cooking something delicious right about now. She loves food as much as I love fishing."

Grandpa stretched out his arms and pointed toward the green meadows and farmland surrounding them. He traced his finger along the river, which snaked its way through the valley.

"This is what I wanted my heaven to be."

"It's wonderful, like nothing I've ever seen," James said. "How long have you been here?"

"It's been some time — maybe over a decade if you do the math, but it feels like it was just yesterday when I arrived. Time ticks differently here. Our souls are no longer bound by earth's revolutions. In heaven, years may only feel like days or even seconds."

Grandpa rubbed his hand in a circular motion across his bulging belly that prevented him from buttoning his fishing vest.

"The stomach cancer that killed me is gone. No more needles. No more suffering. The pain we experience in life doesn't cross the threshold of death. Heaven is filled with only peace and love." He looked up at the palette of colors mixing with the clouds. "I'll never get tired of that sky."

As they had during their fishing trips together, James and Grandpa watched the sun dip below the mountains, leaving behind an explosion of pinks mixing with oranges. They soaked in the beauty of it all before James interrupted the tranquility with a question weighing heavy on his mind.

"Why did I have to die like that?"

Grandpa gestured for James to follow him to the water's edge. The shallow section of the river was only 2 feet deep.

"I know none of this makes any sense, but I promise you'll get the answers you seek. Unfortunately, I'm not the person who can provide them. All you have to know is that you fulfilled your life's journey. But the adventure is not over. There's more to learn. Look into the water."

"I don't see anything."

A school of minnows darted around a maze of riverbed rocks and disappeared into a muddy cloud that was growing larger. The maelstrom picked up speed and a scene emerged at the center of the soupy fog. There were no colors — only black, white and gray. A group of people stood around a rectangular stone

"What's happening?" James asked.

"The river is speaking to you."

Dozens draped in black circled a mahogany coffin.

Their tears mixed with a heavy rainfall. One by one, the mourners left roses on top of the wooden box. The downpour separated the flowers, and wet petals stuck to the casket. A priest wearing a wide-brimmed black hat and a raincoat recited burial prayers and sprinkled holy water, but the fierce winds blew away the droplets before they could land on the grave.

"O God, by whose mercy the faithful departed find rest. Bless this grave and send your holy angel to watch over it."

The crowd responded in unison.

"Amen."

James's parents sobbed and squeezed each other's soaking wet hands. Neither had an umbrella. Their heads were down. Their bodies hunched forward. Despair pulled them into a pit of misery as indescribable pain filled every crevice of their bodies. Somehow, their son had beaten them to the grave. Children weren't supposed to die before their parents.

"Part of your mom and dad died in that crash," Grandpa said. "Time will dull their pain, but there'll always be holes in their hearts."

The downpour flooded the cemetery and forced the procession of mourners to wade through mud and wet grass. Each person touched the obsidian stone with the surname "St. George" etched into the rock. Most dispersed and sought refuge from the storm, but one remained and stood alone from the rest. The expressionless figure leaned up against a birch tree. The leafy canopy provided some protection from the rainfall, but the man curling into the shadow of the branches was still getting soaked.

James's brother Will wanted to cry but couldn't and felt guilty because of it; his body wasn't allowing him to absorb the loss. The pelting rain stung his face. He welcomed the anguish. As long as he felt something, he still knew he was alive. He knelt down into the soaking earth and kissed the wooden box that held what was now a lifeless shell. Two cemetery workers used a crank to lower the casket 6 feet into a murky hole, where it would sit for eternity. They sealed the box in a concrete vault and used shovels to fill the pit with wet dirt. Will's melancholy flowed through James as he watched the burial scene unfold in the muddy swirl in the heavenly river.

"Your brother has been struggling," Grandpa said. "Neighbors and friends have come to your family's home for moral support, hauling trays of lasagna, gourmet sandwiches and meatloaf into the kitchen, but Will locked himself in his room and wouldn't speak to anyone. He'd wanted all of them to go away."

"How could this be happening right now?" James scrunched his face in panic and shook his head. "I died less than an hour ago. Shouldn't I be there to help my brother? I thought you stayed with your loved ones after you died. At least, that's what I read in some book."

"As I mentioned earlier, time moves differently here, and don't worry..."

He gestured back to the cemetery.

"You are *there* helping them."

James scanned the remaining mourners trekking through the grassy deluge and spotted a figure hovering in the shadow of the gravestone. He was the only person not crying. James froze and grabbed Grandpa's arm in surprise.

"How can that be me when I'm here with you?

It's impossible! I can't be in two places at once…
right?"

"Your spirit is everywhere," Grandpa said. "Pieces
of your soul populate the places where your memory
lives, and more often than not, it's with family and
friends. Your energy remains with the ones you left
behind."

James expected to feel bitter about what had
happened — how he died; how he never got to say
goodbye to his parents, his brother and Lily. Instead,
he experienced serenity. The feeling surprised him,
and he couldn't explain why the dread he felt in the
ambulance had all but faded. It was as if the heavenly
sunset dissolved his pain. Still, the answers to his
questions felt as far away as the snow-capped
mountains.

"Would you like to taste some of my famous
lemonade?" Grandpa asked and offered a glass
topped with a lemon slice. He'd seemingly conjured
the concoction out of thin air, but James didn't ask
any questions. This was heaven after all, and he was
thirsty. The swirl in the river had disappeared, so he
turned his attention to the sweet drink.

"I made it myself. I know it's sweet, but that's the
way I like it."

Sugar lingered on James's lips and evoked
memories of their fishing trips on the lake.
Grandpa's cooler always had a canteen filled with *bug
juice* as he called it — a name James loved as a little
boy.

"I forgot how good this tasted," he said.

They sat on rickety-wooden chairs near the river's
edge and caught up on years of lost time. James told
Grandpa about Lily, and her quest to become a nurse.

He talked about the furniture he'd built for their small apartment and the money he'd been saving, ever so slowly, for an engagement ring — a few more months, and he would've reached his goal. He told him about how he'd skip out on classes to go hiking. When snow blanketed the forest, he used snowshoes to scale the icy embankments. He told him about the deep-sea fishing trip to Bermuda. There was the time his parent's neighbor let him drive his prized supercar, a Dodge Viper with white racing stripes. He'd never forget how the rocket ship on wheels hugged the road and roared around sharp turns. He mentioned how his mother rescued a Chihuahua from Tennessee named Gracie. She got her name because the furry animal was found dodging cars along a highway, and by the grace of God, she survived. Grandpa's expressions widened with each tale, and he quizzed James on all of the details.

"How big were the fish? What did you wear to stay warm when you went hiking in the snow? What color was the car? Is Gracie a sweet dog?"

Each memory represented a jewel in a multi-colored necklace that'd taken a lifetime to create, or 23 years in James's case. Some memories, like tearing open presents on Christmas morning or tasting the ocean while snorkeling, were bright pink like rubies, while others were dull like black sapphire. There was the time his dad lost his job or when his mother got Lyme disease or the stack of college-admissions rejection letters that filled his mailbox.

James had lost track of time — a relative concept in heaven, as he was learning — and as he finished the last drop of lemonade, a swooshing sound diverted his attention to the river and a wooden boat.

But instead of cutting through the water, the large vessel glided on top of it and propelled itself without oars, a sail or even a motor.

"Is it going to stop?" James's voice trembled as the boat headed toward them with no signs of slowing down. As it sped closer to the riverbank, the shadows of two, expressionless giants loomed over the meadow. James estimated they were both at least 12 feet tall. Except for their different hair colors, brown and blond, the behemoths were mirror images. Each wore hooded-silk tunics that touched the ground, one a purplish-blue and the other emerald green, and had immense hands with elongated fingers as thick as sausages. The boat came to an abrupt stop within an inch of the shoreline.

"May I introduce Archangels Michael and Raphael," Grandpa said.

The titans stepped onto the riverbank and left foot imprints the size of manhole covers. Their strides were four times longer than the average mortal's, and they climbed the grassy hill in a few swift steps. James arched his neck up at the guardians, waiting for them to speak, but they said nothing. He'd expected more affable temperaments from God's most supreme angels and trustworthy ambassadors. Instead, the archangels bowed in unison and stepped aside to allow a much smaller man to pass in-between.

"Jimmy!" Chuck shouted. "Dude, I'm so happy you're okay!"

The teenage surfer was sporting the same board shorts he wore on the bridge. A small hoop earring dangled from his left lobe.

"Chuck… I don't know… I just…"

"Hey man, you made it! Your destiny led you here.

Man, isn't that, like, so crazy?"

"I have so much to ask that I don't even know where to begin."

"Well, ask away buddy."

"Did I feel any pain when I died?"

"Well... did you?"

"I don't think so."

James rubbed his chest where the car had hit him but felt no cuts or bruises.

"I think I'm okay, but I was hit so hard. I can't remember. I had to feel something, right?"

Chuck shook his head.

"Dude, I was there to help you. Your soul left your body right before the car hit you."

"I don't understand."

"Don't you see?" Chuck flicked back his head to shift his bleached hair poking out from underneath a baseball cap. "I'm your spirit guide, Jimmy. I've been with you since the beginning."

James was stunned.

"That little voice in your head all those years," Chuck said proudly. "Dude, that was me. 'Don't do this. Stay away from that. Maybe I shouldn't go there.' Remember that boat crash?"

How could James forget it? He and two friends had swiped the keys to a speed-boat that belonged to his buddy's dad and went for a late-night joy ride to celebrate their high school graduation. But with only moonlight guiding the way, they didn't see the unlit, construction barge anchored in the middle of the river. All three were tossed from the boat and into the icy water. Somehow, they survived with only a few broken bones and cuts.

"Remember how you ignored your buddy who

told you to sit in the front of the boat? He wanted you to feel the wind, but something inside you thought otherwise. That was me guiding you away from danger. Otherwise, you wouldn't have survived the crash."

James remembered hearing his friends scream for help while they floated in the water. Hypothermia had set in, and his body temperature plummeted. Blood dripped from a cut on his neck. The flashing lights from the approaching patrol boat disoriented him, and he couldn't hear what the officer was shouting. When the patrolman extended his hand, James stared at it, unsure what to do. His mind was frozen. Something told him to grab on, so he did, and was pulled to safety.

"I barely made it out alive."

"But you did, and I was there with you."

James shot Chuck a pained stare.

"How come you didn't protect me on the bridge?"

Chuck's surfer-boy smile faded, and he stepped closer to James.

"Jimmy, it was your time. I can't tell you why. That's not for me to explain, but I promise you'll find out soon."

Reuniting with Chuck felt like discovering a long-lost friend who'd never been lost at all. He was only waiting to be found.

"My destiny was to help you from beginning to end. Man, it was so hard showing you your banged-up body in the ambulance, but you had to see it. Otherwise, you'd be a wandering soul, lost and confused forever."

James held back tears.

"I'm sorry you died, man — especially the way it

happened. Totally awful. It's kind of like the way I went out."

James titled his head.

"How'd you die?"

"Drowned. Riptide carried me out. I was all alone on a break when I lost my board after a wave knocked the heck out of me. Dude, like you, I don't remember much at all, only that it was freaking cold and no one could hear me. I was a good swimmer too, but it's tough treading water in the Pacific. My arms and legs got tired, and I couldn't stay afloat. My body gave out. Jimmy, you understand now why I was your spirit guide? We both had tragic deaths. We both died alone."

James swallowed hard and struggled to speak.

"Don't worry. No need to say anything. You know I'm there for you."

Chuck stuck out his thumb and pinky in a hang-loose gesture and smiled again. Then, he started walking toward the rickety boat bobbing in the river and waved to James to follow.

"Time to take a ride."

"Take a ride?" James asked with an anxious look. "Where are we going?"

"I've got some surfing to do. Man, I've really missed those waves. It's been a long time since I've been in the water, and I've been itching to get back in. I guess it's like what the philosophers say, everything comes full circle — something crazy like that, right? Got to do what I love. Plus, I need to prove I'm not afraid of the ocean. As for you, it's time to get your answers."

Chuck stuck out his palm for a high five, and James reciprocated.

"Will I see you again?"

"Oh yeah!" said Chuck. "I'm sure of it, and if you ever need to find me, look to the ocean. That's where I'll be."

Grandpa, Chuck and the stone-faced archangels escorted James toward the boat.

"Don't be afraid," Grandpa said. "I'm not going anywhere either. There are plenty of fish for me to catch here and one in particular with my name on it."

"But I can't leave you now," James said. "After all these years, I finally found you, and we have so much to talk about."

"It's time to take the next step in your journey or else none of what happened will make sense. I'll be waiting for you when you're done."

James embraced his grandfather one last time before he walked up a rickety plank, which creaked under his weight. Decorative carvings dotted the deck of the boat: a dove carrying an olive branch in its beak; a ship navigating the rough seas and a snake wrapped around a tree, which reminded him of Little Gerry. The archangels followed James onboard.

"Is there anything I should grab onto?" he asked without seeing railings, but neither responded or even acknowledged his presence. James prayed he wouldn't get bucked off into the river.

"Good luck," Grandpa shouted from the riverbank.

James's heart fluttered with apprehension.

Without warning, the vessel lifted out of the water, maneuvered downstream and picked up speed. James couldn't comprehend how the stoic giants propelled the boat at blinding speed. The forest and sapphire sky were replaced by a white tunnel of light. He wanted to ask what was happening but felt too nauseous. Plus, he expected they'd ignore him. Radiance engulfed the boat and flashed like lightning bolts.

CHAPTER 4
SWEET TEA ON THE BEACH

The motley trio jolted to a halt on the sandy shores of a solitary island filled with mangrove trees. Their roots arched high above the salty water and bent downward at a sharp angle like a cricket's leg. The tropical rain forest encircled the base of a volcano. Its summit overlooked a vast ocean with nothing but the horizon in the distance. Glacial clouds cast shadows on the undulating water before drifting and giving way to the sun.

Waves crashed against the side of the wooden boat and sprayed James in the face, burning his eyes. He remembered how he'd blindly smacked his head against the cabinet at the bar the night he died, so he squinted hard and forced himself to tear. No need to get disoriented and stumble overboard.

James assumed the archangels were too tall for the water to reach their faces, but when he checked on his travel companions, he was startled by the creatures standing before him. The archangels were gone, and in their place, sat two gray wolves: light-greenish eyes encircling dark pupils; bushy fur coats; sharp claws and long muzzles with black noses. Their nostrils flared as they sniffed the air and stared curiously at their frightened passenger, who took three steps backward.

"Michael? Raphael?"

His heart beat twice as fast, and his eyes darted from side to side, searching for a quick escape, but there was no way out. The wolf sitting where Raphael once stood arched its back in a stretch and made its way toward James. His shoulder blades moved up and down with each step like pistons in an engine. Streaks of white mixed with gray made up its thick coat. The wolf lifted its rounded nose and sniffed James's fingers before licking them. He breathed a sigh of relief and scratched the top of the animal's head. When standing on all fours, the wolf reached the top of James's hip.

"Thank you for taking me here."

Both wolves laid on the deck and rested their heads on their paws. It was time to leave his furry friends and explore the oasis before him.

"I'm going to take a walk and see what's around. I'll be back in a little bit."

The archangels-turned-wolves looked up sheepishly but otherwise didn't budge. James jumped over the side of the boat and fell several feet before splashing into water as warm as a bathtub. The muscles in his legs loosened. He inhaled the salty air and kicked off his socks and sneakers. His feet squished into the sand, and his big toe pressed against the spiny arm of a starfish. He plucked it from the water and measured the bright-orange disc against the palm of his hand. The starfish was captivating, and he would've spent more time admiring its magnificence, except that it was recoiling in the hot sun, so he put it back on the sea floor.

A school of red fish with yellow tails tickled his feet. Their illuminous colors shimmered underwater. In the distance, silvery tails as big as tractors broke through the water's surface as watery mists shot into the sky. A flock of seagulls squawked at James, who kicked his way through the waves.

A giant sea turtle greeted him on the beach and cranked his centuries-old neck to get a better look at the new visitor. His eyes moved with sloth-like speed. He surveyed James's features, but after finding nothing of interest, the green reptile returned to standing guard before the aquatic menagerie. James brushed his palm across the turtle's elaborate shell, which was divided into boney-brown sections that got lighter as they peaked.

"He's not going to talk to you. I can promise you that. No magical turtles here."

The words weren't spoken directly to James but rather appeared in his mind. He looked up toward the clouds.

"I'm not up there," the bassy voice said. "I've over here, sitting on the beach chair. I've been waiting for you."

Several hundred feet down the beach, James spotted a bald man lounging in a weathered, white wooden chair. The stranger waved and beckoned James to the empty seat next to him.

"Join me and enjoy the show."

James felt himself drawn to the man as if a magnetic force was pulling them together, so he walked toward the chairs but noticed something was following him, albeit something very slow — the sea turtle had become his shadow.

This time, he heard the man's voice as opposed to feeling his words.

"I see Henry has become your new friend."

"Henry?"

"He's been with me for a long time." The man had a wide grin stretching across his face. His chocolaty skin glistened in the heat. A navy linen shirt and white linen pants fluttered in the ocean breeze. He playfully kicked up powdery sand with his bare feet. "Would you like some sweet tea?"

"No thank you. I just had lemonade and am not thirsty," James said.

"Ah, yes — Grandpa's famous lemonade! It's quite good. No disputing that, but I think my sweet tea is better."

The man's satisfied laughter rumbled across the ocean.

"Don't tell Grandpa because I wouldn't want to hurt his feelings. The truth is that I've never been one for the tangy. My penchant is sweetness."

The ice cubes in his glass clanged together. He sipped and savored the sugary drink and chuckled with delight. James was drawn to his cavernous and cerulean eyes, which hid many secrets. His muscular arms filled out his short-sleeve shirt. His long neck elevated a chiseled face that exuded warmth.

"Are you sure you don't want any?"

"Not right now."

"What'd you think of the archangels?"

"I never knew someone could be that tall. To be honest, I don't know what to make of them or any of this."

"I admit that it can all be overwhelming, but you've seen all of this before, including the archangels. You just never opened your eyes to them. There are many different kinds of angels, but the archangels are the generals, so to speak, serving and answering only to me."

James paused, letting several seconds of silence to pass between them.

"Who are you?"

The man wiped away the sweat collecting along his brow and poured another glass of sweet tea.

"I've been called many names since the beginning of time. Far too many to remember or count."

James stared at the man with the inquisitiveness of a child.

"Don't act surprised — you felt my words when you walked along the beach. I'm the omniscient creator. Were you expecting a man with a fluffy beard? Too hot for a beard."

James changed his mind and poured himself a glass of sweet tea, wishing he had some whiskey to add to the mix. His hand shook as he brought the glass to his lips, and he spilled the sugary drink onto the sand. There was so much to ask, but he didn't know where to start.

"Why did I die?" he blurted out, surprised at both his boldness and acerbic tone.

God pursed his lips and put down his glass.

"I don't blame you for starting with the most important question. I'd do the same."

A humpback whale burst through the water and hung in the air before crashing back into the ocean. James tried to appreciate the majestic moment but was distracted by noises in the sand. Henry was still several hundred feet away, making one sluggish step before another, so where were the sounds coming from?

"Ah, you're looking for Little Gerry," God said.

"Little Gerry?" James furled his brow in confusion. "He's here?"

The ball python slithered underneath Jake's chair and curled next to his feet like a puppy. James picked up his pet reptile and plopped him on his lap. He recognized the distinct, scaly patterns on his body.

"Most people associate snakes with Satan, but that's a misguided interpretation," God explained. "The shedding of skin represents rebirth and transformation, much like you're undergoing."

"But how did Little Gerry get here so quickly? I just died... I think."

"Remember what Grandpa told you. Heaven does not adhere to terrestrial time and James..." God stared directly into his eyes. "I am sorry about how you died. Every person deserves dignity in death, but unfortunately, not everyone gets it. Thankfully, Chuck was there to cross you over to the other side. Would you walk with me to the water?"

James nodded and lowered Little Gerry back to the sand.

Together, they strolled over a dune toward the ocean waves. God wasn't as tall as the archangels but still towered over James. His bare feet left large imprints on the beach. Henry, still in the midst of a methodical stroll, changed course and moved in their direction.

"Most people see death as the end but that's an inaccurate perception," God said. "Death is part of your soul's journey. It's the middle rung in a ladder. For some, death comes sooner. For others, death comes during old age. It doesn't mean that a longer life is better than a shorter one. What matters is our soul's path, and more importantly, what we learn from it."

"Why would you allow bad things to happen to people who've lived good lives?" James asked, once again, surprising himself at his boldness. "I'm sorry... I didn't mean to be... I mean..."

"It's okay," God interrupted. "You have a right to ask, and I daresay, be angry too."

"It's just that I don't understand. If you love and care for all living things, why would you allow for bad things to happen to your creations?"

"You won't remember this, but before you were born, your soul and I had a contract of sorts," God explained.

They waded through the waves and watched a starfish roll into the surf, similar to the one James had picked up near the boat. He too felt like a small creature tossed around in a rough current.

"I promised you a life filled with love and family, including selfless parents and a nurturing home. You had the opportunity to learn, grow and fall in love. You met Lily and experienced ineffable joy, but you were also meant to come home sooner, and there's a reason for that. It's all part of your journey. Take a look into the water."

An emerald cloud emerged near their feet, similar to the one Grandpa showed him in the lake, but this underwater formation was saturated with pulsating colors. James saw his parents at a backyard barbeque on a summer day. Wrinkles covered their hands and faces. His father's movements were slower and more deliberate. Gray had invaded his once jet-black hair. While time and loss weighed down his body, he still had a sparkle in his eyes. So did his mother. They were happy about something... about someone.

The giggling infant crawled in a playpen packed with squishy toys. The cherub-like child had strands of curly hair. He laughed and played with an army of stuffed dinosaurs.

Standing nearby, his brother kept one eye on his son and the other on the hamburgers sizzling on the grill. A tall brunette with greenish eyes hugged Will and kissed his cheek.

"This little one moves so fast," his mother said. She cooed at the chubby baby and tickled his belly. "Soon, he'll be walking and then running. You're going to have trouble on your hands."

"A piece of you lives on in that boy," God said. "Will named his son after you."

James's eyes swelled with tears, which rolled down his cheeks and fell into the powdery sand. He knew his death had left an indelible scar on his parents, but maybe his brother's son could heal their wounds and restore normalcy to a family split apart. The melancholy and longing that had weighed him down were gone. He missed his family but found comfort seeing his parents' newfound happiness.

"It hasn't been easy for them," God said. "There've been lots of long days. Without hope, shadows can swallow the soul, but it's important to remember that a single light can dispel darkness."

The emerald cloud at their feet dissolved into the waves, and the giggling baby gave way to coral and rainbow fish.

"Your parents were able to survive the pain because of hope in their hearts. Their journey included a most terrible loss. It'll all make sense to them when they return home to see me."

James inflated his chest with an uncomfortable breath.

"Thank you for showing me that," he said. "But I must admit, you never answered my question."

"Ah, yes — the age-old question! You and I could put a thousand philosophers out of work right now. The truth is no life is without obstacles. Some face greater struggles than others. Some are rich. Some are poor. Some are healthy. Some are sick. Everyone has a lesson to learn. Unfortunately, not everyone learns their lessons. Some souls don't mature, and ignorance leads to poor choices."

"Did I learn my lesson?"

"Your lesson isn't over yet."

A firefly as large as the one that followed James on the old stone bridge landed on God's shoulder. Daylight masked his glow.

"You lived a good life and puts others first. You respected your family and strived to be a better man. Be proud of yourself because I'm proud of what you've accomplished."

James locked on to God's every word.

"I want to offer you something special, something that will dictate your destiny — no pressure here."

God flashed his pearly-white teeth.

"You deserve better than how you died, which is why you've earned the right to choose your next adventure."

"My next adventure?"

"As I gave mankind free will, I also give you a

most-important choice. You can remain here in paradise with Grandpa. Heaven is a wondrous place that cannot be described in words and must be felt in the heart. In time, your family will join you — your parents, your brother and Lily — and as you wait for them, you'll live peacefully and devoid of any sorrow because paradise is without sadness.

"Or, you can start anew and be reborn into a loving family. Your life will be healthy and prosperous. It's a chance to have the experiences you were deprived of, like getting married, having children and growing old. They're life's greatest treasures. Your soul will always remain connected to your current family, but you'll be adding new family members too. Love is an unbreakable bond that not even death can shatter. After you live a full life and cross over again, you'll be reunited with both families."

James didn't know how to respond. In truth, he felt cheated out of his dreams. There was still so much he wanted to do. However, heaven was beyond compare. A refuge without suffering. A world shaped by imagination. A place of dreams.

"But there's something else," said God, who peered over at the rickety boat where the wolves were standing guard. The vessel rocked in the waves and looked less seaworthy from afar.

"There are many angels inhabiting this celestial realm, and they take many different forms. Angels are the intermediaries connecting two worlds. They engender peace whenever evil is present. Unfortunately, there is a never-ending battle between good and evil."

God took a few steps into the sea and a bright-white light hovered around his feet.

"Angels are born of the light and have never had a human experience, but in some rare instances, souls can become angels, an honor only a select few are offered."

James felt God's voice in his head again. His heart tingled with excitement.

"Do you understand what I'm offering?"

James was quiet.

"This is a chance to serve," God said. "I'm giving you an opportunity to earn that honor. It's a task with great responsibility, but as is the case with most things, you must prove you deserve it."

"What do I have to do?"

"You'll face an arduous test and dare I say an epic adventure. Only once you complete this trial will you earn the honor to join my service. I understand why you wouldn't want to do this, but nothing worth doing is easy."

The white light in the water surrounding God's feet grew brighter and more blinding.

"If you so desire to be a being of light, you must be a beacon of light for another."

"Like Chuck did for me?"

"Just like Chuck did, except you'll be responsible for both protecting and guiding a soul. Think of it as a cross between a guardian angel and a spirit guide."

"Would I be alone?" A flurry of butterflies filled James's stomach. "Will you be there to help me? I wouldn't even know where to begin."

"If you accept this arduous task, you must do it alone. It won't be easy, and you'll be tested every step of the way. It could take many years to complete, and there's no guarantee of success."

The gravity of James's choice weighed heavy on his heart. As foreign as heaven was, it still felt like home, and he envisioned himself happy waiting to greet his family. While the prospect of experiencing a new life was exciting, starting over meant losing an identity he'd come to cherish, and James had no interest in doing that. His heart belonged to Lily, and he didn't want to share it with another.

"Let the light guide your decision because in my light, you will always see truth," said God, who disappeared into the aquatic tornado building beneath him, leaving only a lingering radiance in the water. The wolves and the rickety boat were gone too.

James was alone.

He stood before a myriad of sea life that swirled around the beckoning underwater glow and dragged his hand across the energy pulsating in the surf. The healing water relaxed his fingers and calmed his soul. He felt the ocean summoning him, so he submerged his body into the luminescence. His head stopped aching, and he'd forgotten about the enormous choice before him.

Schools of radiating maroon fish surrounded his rejuvenated body. A stingray jutted toward him, stopped mere inches from his face, and motioned with its rippling body for James to follow. Its tail whipped around and moved toward a purple bubbling hole in the ocean floor. A benevolent force pulled him into the violet light where warm bubbles shot out of the circular cavity.

James spotted a reflection of his mother's sleeping face in the effervescence. She looked as she had the last time he saw her, but when he tried to touch her cheek, he couldn't reach, so he swam into the hole against the flow of the bubbles to get closer. It felt like passing through a funnel of fizz. The bubbles numbed his face. His body floated down the underwater cavity.

When he finally came to, James found himself standing next to his parents' bed. Both his mom and dad were fast asleep underneath their blankets. He leaned over and kissed his mother and father on their cheeks. During their senior years, their fading memories alleviated some of their pain, allowing them to catch up on years of lost sleep.

"I love you both," he whispered. "I didn't mean for any of this to happen. If only I knew what I know now, I wouldn't have walked home across the bridge."

For the briefest of moments, his parents came to and opened their glassy eyes, but neither could make out the blurred face at the edge of the bed.

"Is that you, James?" his mother asked.

He put his hand on his mother's forehead.

"Mom, heaven is the most beautiful place. I met Grandpa there."

"We miss you," his father said. "Come back to us."

"I know, but I can't. I have to go back. It's not yet time for us to be together, but I promise we'll be together again, and I'll keep visiting in your dreams. The stingray led me here."

His mother smiled.

"I asked him to bring you to me. He's been in my dreams. There was also a tropical island where the water and sky are the same color, and the sea is filled with whales and dolphins. There's even a volcano that climbs into the clouds."

He kissed his mother's cheek again, and she fell back into a deep slumber. So did his father. James's hazy late-night visit would provide much comfort to his mourning parents for years to come. Their son had come back to see them and that's all that mattered. A sliver of moonlight dashed across their bed.

James stepped back into the shadows. God was right. He was blessed to have loving parents. Seeing them at peace, however fleeting, provided some solace. They'd be okay, and one day, they'd be together again.

His mother had always encouraged him to accept challenges with open arms. "You won't grow unless you push yourself," she'd say. James thought he hadn't pushed himself enough during his life and never tested his limits. He ignored the road less traveled and preferred the paved path. It wasn't until he fell in love with Lily that his outlook changed, but by then, it was too late.

Yes — it was time for a new adventure. Time to realize his full potential and pursue his destiny. James wanted to be proud of his accomplishments. He was in the process of making that happen when he died on the bridge.

He stared at his parents curled up in their bed, closed his eyes and fell back into the purple light.

CHAPTER 5
FROZEN HELL

A biting chill stung James's face and penetrated his skin down to the bone. His jaw throbbed. His teeth chattered. Cold dampness enveloped his body. He stared out at the world through a tiny square window, and the crescent moon stared back before a cloudy mist shrouded its silvery hue and swallowed the surrounding stars. The wind whistled past his ear and carried the distant pleas of tortured souls wailing in the night.

A fluorescent lightbulb housed inside a plastic encasing covered in dust flickered in the darkness. Its buzz echoed in the space, a hum that could drive a person insane.

Melancholy seeped into James like a cancer, and he couldn't get rid of it. The depressive feeling crippled his body. Whatever warm contentment he'd felt on the sandy beaches of paradise had evaporated inside this sanitized dungeon. He felt as if he'd been dropped in a barrel of ice-cold water, and the shock paralyzed his core.

A spidery shadow crawled against the cinderblock and inched its way toward him. The silhouette on the wall had no discernible features except skeletal arms and legs. Streams of smoke poured from its nostrils. Its survival depended on the flickering ceiling fixture; it disappeared and re-emerged in the dim light.

The shadow's arms reached for a metal pipe that stretched along the ceiling. It hovered around the cylinder and balanced atop a squeaky chair, similar to one James had built in the carpenter's shop. White paint chips rained onto the concrete floor. James crouched down and braced for whatever was to come his way. He squinted in the darkness but could see little, aside from a carving of flames etched into the back of the chair. Someone had used a crude knife to create the image.

James wondered if God had tricked him into coming to this forbidden hell; maybe he'd made a terrible choice leaving heaven. His nervous thoughts were interrupted by a slamming noise followed by choking and gasping. The confluence of sounds echoed against the decaying walls. The wooden chair crashed onto its side and splintered into shards, and above it, two legs bicycle-kicked, searching for a surface that was no longer there. The shadow squirmed like a freshly punctured worm on a fishing hook. Spit shot to the ground. The dim glow from the overhead light burned to a near blip, until... there was nothing.

A throbbing pain jolted James's heart. His breathing slowed and the muscles in his neck constricted. Tighter and tighter. A dejected heaviness weighed down his soul. He didn't know where these despondent feelings had come from but knew he had to do something to break the spell. He leapt toward the dangling thing in distress, unsure of what he'd find in the darkness, and bear-hugged an emaciated man. Baggy jeans slid down the twiggy legs and over yellow toenails as sharp as razor blades. Bare feet jerked up and down until they were motionless.

The gurgling stopped, and the room fell back into eerie silence The skeleton hung like frozen beef in a meat locker. James grabbed the cold feet and heaved upward, but despite being only skin and bone, the body was still too heavy to lift. Blood vessels bulged along the stranger's neck where the bedsheet-turned-noose constricted the windpipe. The knot tightened each time James lifted the body. He could feel the grim reaper's presence; a dark figure waiting in the corner, tapping his fingers, counting the seconds.

James blindly stuck out his arms and searched the room for anything he could stand on to get closer to the ever-tightening knot. There wasn't much in the frozen space except for a rickety bed frame with a compressed mattress. He brushed his hand across the rusted metal and cob webs ensnared his fingers. James dragged the bedframe toward the middle of the room. Its corroded legs scraped the concrete floor. The ancient coils supporting the mattress squeaked as he climbed on top of it.

Darkness shrouded the lifeless face, and gray hair covered the man's eyes. Like a suffocating goldfish, his mouth was opened wide in a last-ditch effort to suck in air. The bedsheet was cutting off oxygen to his lungs. Veins ballooned and pulsated from a pasty neck. His muscles gave up, and his head limped forward. Arms and legs went limp.

The clouds blocking the crescent moon faded, and silvery light poured back into the square room through the window fortified with bars. The corroded cylinders casted a crisscross pattern on the body swaying from the water pipe.

James's efforts to untangle the knot had proved fruitless. He turned his head away in disgust. No sense watching a man die when there's no way to help.

It was like the time he went bow-hunting with Grandpa — his first and last hunt. The eight-point buck walked across a blanket of crunchy leaves, while James and Grandpa used a patch of birch trees as cover. Both wore camouflage and blended into the landscape. Grandpa maneuvered underneath a raspberry bush with ninja-like precision. Without even clipping a branch, Grandpa raised his bow, notched the feathered arrow, aimed at the moving target, held his breath and fired. The arrow stuck the buck in the heart, and he screamed out, something James wasn't expecting. But instead of falling to the earth in a silent death, the deer made a clumsy attempt at an escape. He galloped over roots and brush before slamming into a trees. Grandpa fired two more arrows, and the buck surrendered on the forest floor.

James felt helpless. The animal's obsidian eyes gazed back at his attackers in puzzled pain, wondering why they'd shot him. Grandpa used every part of that deer, and the meat lasted for weeks, but James would never forget the powerless feeling of not being able to help the suffering animal.

The memory distracted him from what the

moonlight had uncovered among the dust balls on the cold floor. A corroded screw shimmered in the light. Its threads were rusty but still sharp. It must have fallen out of the bedframe, he thought. James scooped up the metal and pressed it between his fingers like a miniature saber. Yes — this would work.

He forced its point into the linen and tore its threads. The hole grew larger as the man's body weight pulled apart the bedsheet. The skeleton plunged to the floor and landed with a thud. His head smacked against the ground. He was unconscious. The white sheet was soaked in spit.

No breathing. No motion. No life.

Is he dead?

James worked fast to remove the noose. The man's skin immediately turned pink as blood flowed back through the veins in his neck. Still, he lay immobile on the ground.

The fluorescent lightbulb buzzed back to life. Its yellowy glow illuminated more of the decrepit room, including a series of tally marks carved into the wall underneath the window. A crack ran across the middle of the floor and underneath a sink caked in dust. The hot water handle was missing. A bar of hardened soap had grown into the side of the ceramic. The toilet was without a seat cover, and a piece of string tied to a lever was the only way to flush. A piece of rectangular metal bolted to the wall acted as a de facto desk. Cobwebs covered the leather binding of an unopened bible, but the book's presence did little to dispel the evil permeating the space. Demons lurked in the shadows, and James could feel them. They connived to weaken the inhabitant of the prison cell and had nearly succeeded in luring their prey into eternal abyss.

It was unclear if the unconscious person would survive. James leaned over and pressed his ear to the man's parched lips covered in blisters. He heard faint, shallow breaths. James used his thumb to lift the man's right eyelid and found a dilated pupil surrounded by a hazel iris.

He fell backward in stunned silence. He'd seen those eyes before.

The man's face had aged — more wrinkles on the brow and moles on the cheeks — but those distinctive green eyes were the same. When James saw them on the old stone bridge, they were bloodshot and swollen. Now, they were glassy and unresponsive.

The prostrated man sprawled out on the damp floor was the cause of all of his pain, responsible for ending James's life and creating lifetime misery for his family. His poison had been mixed drinks and whisky shots. His weapon was a two-door, fire-engine coupe. James had happened to be in the crosshairs. If only he'd spent a few extra minutes cleaning up at the bar, maybe he could have dodged fate's evil surprise.

Wrath flowed through his arms and into his fingertips. The gutless coward deserved no sympathy. He couldn't even take his punishment like a man. Here he was trying to cheat his way out of serving his sentence.

Once muscular with a broad chest and bulging arms, Prisoner #1030 (as indicated by the numbers printed on the back of his prison-issued shirt) was gaunt. Gone were the preppy polo and khaki shorts.

James grabbed the iron bars separating the cell from a long corridor and squeezed until his knuckles turned white. He tried to rip the metal from the concrete, but the bars wouldn't budge. Light shined through a glass window in a metal security door at the end of the hallway. There were cells on either side but all were dark, and James couldn't see into any of them.

"Why are you torturing me?" he shouted.

Silence.

"I want to come back."

More silence.

He sucked in the dry chill. It burned his nostrils. The scrawny man in a fetal position on the ground moaned and clutched his bloodied neck. The torn, white sheet lay at his feet, evidence of his failed suicide.

"Can't even kill myself," he muttered.

Tears streamed down his cheeks in a deluge of misery that mixed with blood on his swollen lips. He smashed his fists into the ground with fury and hoped he'd break the bones in his hands. He needed to feel something — anything.

"I deserve to die."

Prisoner #1030 pointed his watery eyes at James, who studied his killer's weathered face. Thinning gray strands had replaced what was once thick-brown hair. His expression was listless. His eyes hollow. For what felt like an eternity, the two stared at each other — the killer and his victim face-to-face — in what was a one-way mirror. While the defeated man in the gray jumpsuit couldn't see his spirit guide in the physical world, he felt an unusual energy manifesting inside his prison cell. The hairs on his neck stood tall.

He knew he wasn't alone.

CHAPTER 6
DEMONS EVERYWHERE

Victor Young stood out in the exercise yard like a puzzle piece that didn't fit. He shuffled through the dirt in oversized clothes and kept his eyes to the ground, occasionally glimpsing up at the sea of inmates surrounding him, wondering if the waves would come crashing in.

Some convicts at the Watermill Correctional Facility lifted crude dumbbells in an area cordoned off for makeshift fitness equipment. The top of a metal filing cabinet formed the basis of a bench press. The free weights were so corroded that the numbers indicating pounds had faded, so it was anyone's guess as to much each weighed. The chin-up bar had been welded from discarded pipes similar to the one Victor used to try to hang himself.

In another area, a group of ten inmates played pickup basketball on uneven blacktop partially invaded by weeds. They were careful not to bounce the ball on a crack or risk losing it out-of-bounds.

The three-point and foul lines had worn away, and the rims were bent to an 80-degree angle; the warden had no intention of replacing them. Other inmates tossed around a semi-deflated football. They'd let the air out of the pigskin because it was the only way to grip it. Otherwise, the leather was too worn down.

The non-athletic convicts chatted and puffed on cigarettes they'd bought at the commissary or smuggled in as contraband. A loosie was a precious commodity behind bars. Single cigarettes cost as much as 50 cents to a dollar depending on the brand. Inmates used them to bribe guards for just about anything. Three loosies would buy more time on the phone. A half-dozen cigarettes could get extra food in the dining hall. Two dozen might mean shower time alone. But securing a single cell without a roommate required a currency of the financial variety. Anything could be bought in prison with the right bribe.

"Rough night, Young?" a bald, tattooed inmate shouted at Victor, who was walking alone near the security fence. "How'd you get all them scrapes on your neck? Someone put a dog collar on you?"

The inmate's two companions laughed at Victor, who shot them an icy stare but soon realized his mistake and looked the other way. No need to "start something" as they'd say in prison, especially true without allies and protection, and Victor Young had neither.

James wandered a short distance behind Prisoner #1030, unsure what to do. God had told him his responsibility was to guide and protect, but he couldn't bring himself to let go of his anger. He seethed whenever he looked at the man who killed him — a pathetic waste of life who belonged among the miscreants and murderers. Plus, there wasn't much life left in Victor; James could see the light fading in his listless eyes.

After counting the tally marks on the prison cell wall, James calculated Victor had been incarcerated for exactly 5 years and 10 days. Victor had been keeping track because there wasn't much else to do in prison but count things: days behind bars; days until the next appeal; days until a parole board hearing; days in the infirmary after an ambush. A jury had sentenced him to 20 years for vehicular homicide and DUI manslaughter. He'd have to serve 80 percent of his time before being eligible for parole — 11 more years to go.

During the trial, Victor had sat stone-faced next to his lawyer, while the assistant district attorney argued a case based on the facts. The driver's blood alcohol content was .15 — nearly twice the legal limit in New York State. Several witnesses, including an elderly woman who was walking her Papillion at the time of the crash, described in court the collision on the old stone bridge.

"I heard the explosion after the car passed me," she testified.

"Explosion, ma'am?" the prosecutor asked.

"Oh, yes! It sounded like bomb went off. It was so loud that I thought the bridge had fallen into the water. I'll never forget it. Peppy jumped three feet into the air and wouldn't stop barking. He got so scared. I knew something terrible had happened."

"Did you walk over to the bridge to see what terrible thing had happened?"

"Objection, your honor," the defense shouted.

"Sustained," the judge ruled. "Counsel, please rephrase your question."

"My apologies your honor. Did you walk over to the bridge to see what had happened?"

"Oh, yes — I saw the car all busted up. It didn't even look like a car, and the burning was an awful smell. I prayed no one was hurt. When I found out that poor fellow died, I crossed myself and said a prayer."

The state's case was a slam-dunk, and Victor's lawyer, Reeve Rivers, knew it. Rivers's polyester pinstriped suit hugged his slender frame. Globs of gel kept each strand of jet-black hair firmly in place. His tie knot was two sizes too big. A law school class ring as large as a coffee mug hung from his finger. Victor refused to ask his attorney about it, preferring not to further inflate his oversized ego. He wondered if Rivers had learned anything substantial in school because he was clumsy in court and rarely cross-examined any witnesses.

Victor's father-in-law, also a lawyer, had recommended Rivers, who was known for his skill at negotiating reasonable plea deals. Whatever legal relationships Rivers had engendered had been fortified in the bar across the street from the courthouse and lubricated with whisky. He bought top-shelf liquor for all of the judges, and his generosity curried favor in the courtroom and made up for his legal ineptitude.

Unfortunately for Victor, prosecutors had little appetite for a deal. Rivers approached the district attorney about his client pleading guilty to lesser charges, but the state balked. The case would be an easy victory for a district attorney needing to appear tough on crime during a tight re-election bid.

For all of his shortcomings, Rivers tried to plant seeds of doubt in the jurors' minds. His strategy swayed from blaming a sticky accelerator pedal for the crash to reproaching the police for botched accident-reconstruction diagrams and failed breathalyzer tests — it'd taken responding officers three attempts to get an accurate reading. Two hours later, nurses at the hospital drew Victor's blood, and that's when authorities were able to determine that he was legally drunk.

"If the breathalyzer properly worked on the bridge, I'm convinced Victor Young's blood alcohol level would've been higher," the prosecutor argued.

"Objection!" Rivers shouted. "Speculation."

"Sustained," the judge said.

Rivers also censured police for failing to obtain surveillance video. A deli, barber shop, restaurant and motel all had security cameras pointed in the direction of the old stone bridge, but none were checked for footage.

"Securing surveillance video is *Investigation 101*. When the police *finally* realized their error several days later, it was too late," Rivers told the jury. "The video had been recorded over, and now, we'll never know exactly what happened on that bridge."

Yes — surveillance video had been erased. Yes — the investigation was sloppy. Yes — breathalyzer tests had been botched. But the facts pointed to a harsh conclusion: Victor Young drove drunk and killed a 23-year-old man, who was walking to his truck after work.

The jury reached a verdict in less than an hour. They would've finished sooner, but Juror #11 needed to use the bathroom, Jurors #3 and #7 napped as they waited for their colleague to return, and the remaining jurors worried they'd anger the judge if they returned to the courtroom too soon. Maybe he'd think they hadn't given the defendant a fair shake and would order them to continue deliberations, but their minds were made up — guilty on all counts, including felony assault on a law enforcement officer for shoving an arresting officer.

"The good news is that you won't have to serve all 20 years," Rivers told Victor following the trial. "They'll shave time off for good behavior, so there's light at the end of the tunnel."

The cocky attorney beamed and waited for praise from his client, who failed to see the silver lining. Victor wanted to punch his lawyer in the face.

"I deserve my sentence for hiring an attorney named Reeve Rivers," he said. "It's a name straight out of a comic book!"

Rivers's plastic grin faded.

"I know you think you're getting a raw deal, but like I said, you'll get out sooner than you think. If I was a betting man, and you know I am…" Rivers broke into a short laughing spell. "I'd wager you'll be out in 15 years, plus or minus, and don't worry…" Rivers raised his voice in a condescending tone as though he were talking to an infant. "No one is going to forget about you. We'll all come to visit. You'd like that, right?"

"I'm still confused as to why I should be happy about this. I'm going to prison! I hired *you* to keep me out of prison, and *you* failed me!"

Reeves puffed on his cigarette and blew away a cloud of smoke.

"I did my best, buddy, but sometimes, no matter how you spin it, a jury won't buy what you're selling." Another puff on the Marlboro. Victor wondered how Rivers was he able to keep his teeth so white with all that smoking. "But hey, no need to thank me for doing my best."

Rivers smiled again, and his teeth shined as brightly as his gold watch. For the second time in less than five minutes, Victor wanted to punch his lawyer in the face — maybe even take out a few chicklets in the process — but he refrained. No need to irk the judge and give him a reason to tack on more years. He wondered how much of his retainer had paid for Rivers's expensive timepiece. The audacious attorney flaunted the watch in the courthouse holding cells. It's second hand moved with fluidity and glided past the numerical markings embedded in the black face. If only Victor could speed up time and fast-forward through the horror that awaited him. If only he could reverse time and alter the course of his fate.

"You okay, buddy?" Rivers asked with a sly grin.

"Fine!" Victor said. "I'm... just...fine."

"I'll sneak you some liquor when you're in the slammer."

He never did.

"You might actually enjoy the quiet time and being away from it all. Heck, I wish I had as much alone time. The guards will take care of you. I'll make sure of it."

He never spoke to the guards.

"For God's sakes, you're a teacher and not some degenerate with face tattoos."

"Not yet," Victor said.

"Look — they're not going to throw you to the

dogs. They'll watch out for you. The guards like straight-edge guys like you. They know the crash wasn't intentional. You didn't mean to kill someone. That's why they call it an accident! Make the best of the life you've got left. The warden is a friend of mine, a drinking buddy. What's his name? Hamcock? Hamilton? Something like that. I see him at the bar every now and then. I'll talk to him."

Rivers smiled again.

Victor thought it a shame that his lawyer was standing several feet from the cell bars because he really wanted to shatter his jaw. The wily attorney probably knew where to position himself following prior jailhouse altercations with dissatisfied clients.

At the time, Victor wondered if Rivers was sleeping with his wife. There were no facts to back up that idea, just an uncomfortable, innate feeling. Rivers seemed like the type who'd steal another man's spouse at an opportune moment. He wondered if Rivers purposefully delivered a sub-par performance in court to get the incarcerated husband out of the way. And after Victor got his wife's hand-written letter six weeks later, his suspicions were confirmed:

Dear Victor,

Word cannot describe the emptiness I feel. My heart aches for you. I fear for your safety and worry about the dangers awaiting you. I wish I could take you to a faraway place where we could both be happy again. It's a distant dream that gives me comfort on lonely nights.

Despite how I crave your touch, I can't bring myself to forgive you for what you've done, and I don't think I ever will. How could you so recklessly take a life? You destroyed a family and broke so many hearts, mine included. That young man you killed could have been our child.

Sadness has crippled me. Everything we built together crumbled in one drunken night. The foundation of our relationship that we've spent years building together has shattered, and there's no way to put the pieces back together.

There's so much I want to say, so much you need to hear, but when I sat down to write this letter, I was overcome with anger.

It's time for me to say goodbye. It's time for a fresh start. I'd tell you where I'm going, but I don't want you following me when you get out.

There's something else. I've fallen in love with another. He's caring, tender and understanding. We met at the courthouse during the trial. He's a lawyer and was there working on a case. I know he can care for me and that we'll be happy together. This is a chance for me to have a new life.

I'm sorry for breaking your heart, but you've broken mine. I hope our memories give you comfort during the days ahead.

Love,

Kristen

His wife never explicitly said Rivers was her lover, but Victor knew his intuition was correct. It didn't matter much anyway. Apathy and depression had overtaken him. Surviving prison was no longer a priority. Death was a welcomed end. The stone walls, barbed wire and chain-linked fences made him feel less like a man with each passing day.

"A life for a life," he told himself when he tightened the bedsheet around his neck. "It seems like a fair trade."

Back at the prison yard, James watched the inmates harass Victor.

"Come over here," the bald, burly inmate yelled. The words gargled out of his mouth from the pit of his slimy throat. He spit black saliva colored by the chewing tobacco tucked between his gums and cheek. The dip had stained his few remaining teeth brown.

All three inmates wore sleeveless T-shirts to showcase elaborate tattoos snaking from their hands up to their necks. The bald convict had a rippling Confederate flag etched onto his bicep. His friend had a barking bulldog wrapped in chains on his left forearm. But the third man looked like a demon roaming the earth. His entire face was needled in ink to mimic a skeleton. Black colored the areas around his nose and eyes. Lines along his cheeks and jaw gave the illusion of bones, including a set of teeth drawn above and below his lips. The inmates called him Bones. Some thought he was the grim reaper sent to do the devil's bidding.

Bones didn't speak. Some thought him mute, but not the liquor store clerk he'd robbed and butchered with a hatchet. Following a frantic search for the killer, the sheriff cornered the tattooed maniac after spotting the clerk's stolen convertible in a nearby fast-food parking lot. The white leather seats were smeared in blood. Bones smirked when deputies surrounded the vehicle and drew their guns. On the passenger seat, investigators found cash, a roll of quarters and two bottles of whisky. He never explained why he did it.

Bones was among two dozen inmates who aligned themselves with a white supremacist prison gang, thereby enjoying all associations and privileges, including the protection of the bald inmate known as Little Kip, but there was nothing little about him.

"We've been knowing each other for some time now, wouldn't ya say?" Little Kip said to Victor.

At 6 feet 8 inches and 300 pounds, Little Kip towered over everyone at Watermill, including the guards, who'd clutched their weapons in his presence. It would take more than a few shots to bring down the leviathan of a man. Little Kip consumed fear like a nourishing energy. His bare hands were the size of kitchen plates. A black patch covered his right eye, which he'd lost in a cafeteria brawl. A rival gang member had stabbed him in the face with a fork and pierced his pupil, but the injury failed to slow down the giant. After removing the metal utensil from his bloody eyeball, Little Kip wrapped his claw of a hand around the assailant's neck and squeezed until his airway closed. With the melee spreading throughout the cafeteria, the guards couldn't get to the chocking inmate fast enough and relinquish him from the death grip. The goliath squeezed until bones snapped. The fork-wielding attacker died on the linoleum tile.

Little Kip's southern twang was his only link to his past, but he never talked about where he was from, or how he'd made his way north. Whatever happened before prison didn't matter much: with two consecutive life sentences for murder, prison was his permanent home.

"Can't change the past," he'd say.

An unsuccessful bank robbery led to his capture. A teller and two customers ignored his orders to "set down and shut up." When they surreptitiously reached for the manager's desk phone, they were unaware that Little Kip was watching. He used a sawed-off shotgun to silence them — forever.

"They shoulda' listened to me," he said to his masked partner.

Unlucky for Little Kip, the cannon-like blasts piqued the interest of officers responding to another call in the neighborhood. They ambushed the giant in the bank parking lot. He survived three gunshots to the arms and chest. His scrawnier partner did not.

"How'd you get them marks on your neck?" Little Kip asked Victor, who ignored the question.

"Do the world a favor next time you try to off yourself and actually get it done. If you want, I could do it for you. Heck, it don't matter much to me. I'm stuck here, and I haven't had a good killing in some time. I can make it quick too. One crack and you'll be done. Think of it as a favor. You can pay me back on the other side."

"Maybe next time I'll give you a call," Victor said coldly.

James was surprised at Victor's audacity. While he knew he couldn't be seen, even the spirit guide cowered before the men.

"You forgettin' something important. You only still alive because we... excuse me... I let you be. You don't want bad things to happen to you, right?"

Victor knew *bad things* included endless possibilities. When sadistic psychopaths are housed under one roof with endless time on their hands, nightmares become reality. He'd never believed human beings were inherently evil, but he'd come to accept that some were capable of awful things — himself included. It's why he was the only inmate at Watermill who believed he deserved to be there.

"The only reason we watch your back is because you one of us." Little Kip grabbed Victor's shirt and pulled him closer. "We better than they are. We are the superior race."

Victor starred incredulously into the eye — the one without the patch — of the tattooed giant. His face was mere inches from his. Bullies never scared him. Neither did white supremacists covered in blotchy ink. Fear had dissipated long ago because Victor no longer valued life. Once the fear of death is gone, there's little that engenders trepidation.

Little Kip pushed Victor backwards, and he fell hard on the dirt and rocks. The thud sent plumes of dust into the air.

"You pitiful. Best to contribute to the cause, or else we won't protect you no more."

The tattooed skeleton inched closer. His beady eyes zeroed in on the diminutive man in the dirt. Both James and Victor shivered. The warning was clear. The trio turned their backs on the former teacher and walked away.

What "contributing" meant remained unclear, but Victor imagined it involved cash, something he didn't have much of. There was little money in his commissary account. Most of his family and friends had abandoned him years ago — not much love for a drunk-driving murderer. When his wife left him, she took everything, including their life savings and the house. The divorce papers came in a brown envelope alongside the Dear John letter. He didn't have the energy to fight it, so he signed the documents and mailed them back.

Prior to his life behind bars, Victor worked as a high school teacher, respected by his students and adored by his wife, also a teacher. She taught math. He taught English. During lunch, they'd sneak into the janitor's closet and kiss until the bell rang. Her blond hair felt like soft yarn. Her milky skin was smooth. She smelled like roses. They'd planned to start a family one day.

All of their dreams squandered because of beer and whiskey.

CHAPTER 7
CAFETERIA POISON

The servers slopped what resembled food onto plastic plates. The culinary choices included watered-down mashed potatoes, stale cornbread, and a mystery meat with a rubbery texture topped with a reddish sauce. The cook believed salt was the secret ingredient to making any dish tasty, which explained why the inmates kept refilling their water pitchers. But no matter how bad the flavors, the hungry men ate everything.

"Give me some of that extra good stuff, right there," one inmate said to a man wearing a hairnet, smock and rubber gloves. The servers were inmates too because everyone in prison was assigned a work responsibility, but this particular server was uninterested in both the job and the request from the man holding out his food tray.

"I said extra meat!" the inmate demanded again.

A guard who overheard the confrontation flashed his wooden nightstick. Food request denied. Conversation over. The server smirked.

Like everything at Watermill, meal time included strict schedules and protocols. Inmates waited in the same line at the same time every day for breakfast, lunch and dinner. Appetite or no appetite, kitchen staff dumped the awful-tasting cooking on plates divided into three equal sections. However, the partitions did little in preventing the food from merging into a blob.

"Lot of winners in here," James whispered to Victor.

But there was no need to whisper. Victor couldn't hear his spirit guide — at least not yet. James was still adapting to his inconspicuous role as a voiceless man in a world that ignored him. Other inmates were also unaware of his presence. One convict walked right through him. James shut his eyes tight and embraced for the collision but instead found himself standing upright. He smiled — so there are advantages to being dead.

Watermill's finest came from all walks of life. There were rapists, murderers, thieves, cheats and gamblers, who'd do it all again if they had the chance. All of them broke bread together in one giant hall filled with long tables and benches.

Victor stood out among the motley mix of miscreants. He was an educated loner, a teacher turned killer, no gang affiliation, no table to sit at, not a friend in the world. His good behavior curried favor with the guards, and after his roommate Joey overdosed in the bathroom, they allowed Victor to live alone in his double-bed cell in the older section of the penitentiary.

Joey was a heroin supplier from Staten Island, who'd used boats to carry product across New York Harbor to Manhattan. His luck ran out when a Coast Guard vessel intercepted one of his shipments. After he was arrested and sent to Watermill, he became more interested in using heroin than selling it and tried to entice his new roommate to join him.

"Try some, man, I promise it'll make the pain go away," he told Victor. "The divorce, the crash, the money, the guilt — it fades just like magic!"

But Victor had no interest in shooting heroin, nor drinking alcohol ever again. Ultimately, Joey's addiction overcame him, and he died six months into Victor's stint. The guards decided it was safer to leave Victor in his own cell than risk bunking him with another gang-banger or drug slinger. At first, he found the solitary space a refuge from a world of chaos, but over time, the walls closed in and demons got the upper hand.

"Remember, no peanuts," Victor mumbled to the server. "I'm allergic."

"Whatever," the server said and dumped what resembled a peanut butter and jelly sandwich on his plate.

Something wasn't right. James sensed danger but was unsure what engendered the anxious feelings.

"I think… I don't know… but I feel like we should leave," James said.

An inmate sitting at a nearby table had overheard the conversation about the food allergy and shouted at Victor.

"You gonna eat that?" he asked. "Come over here and join us."

The inmate was in his late 20's and had a trimmed beard that highlighted a chiseled chin and complemented an afro. A shiny gold tooth with a diamond lightning bolt glistened underneath the harsh lights of the dining hall. The dental accessory had earned him the nickname Goldie — a far cry from his given name, Winston Victorians, which lacked the same street appeal.

Like everyone else, Goldie wore the same drab jumpsuit, but his clothes weren't faded, torn or tattered. They were new and pressed. He had a leather bracelet on his left wrist and a gold ring with an emerald stone on the middle finger of his right hand. Jewelry was a violation at Watermill, but Goldie had bribed the guards. When he spoke, a cadre of criminal acolytes surrounding the young gang-banger stopped talking and gave him their undivided attention.

"Don't sit down," James warned. He was taken back by his concern for Victor's well-being. "This doesn't feel right. Something is wrong." But Victor, who often ate meals alone, ignored James's plea and took a seat next to the stranger.

"Peanut butter and jelly is my favorite," Goldie said. He snatched the sandwich from Victor's plate and pulled apart the two slices of bread to inspect its contents. "On this side, you got crunchy peanut butter. Pretty simple really. Plain and boring. Most people like it, except you, of course, because you allergic. I heard what you said to the server."

Goldie's snake-like eyes darted from one member of his crew to another and then back to Victor. An uneasy feeling crawled up James's leg. He was unsure how to warn Victor, whose melancholy had formed an impenetrable barrier to the energy around him.

"On the other slice of bread, you got jelly — my favorite part of the sandwich," Goldie continued. He smashed the two slices of rye together and took a generous bite. His gold tooth glimmered as he chomped up and down, and his beady eyes remained in constant motion.

"Life is filled with metaphors," he continued. "Look at it this way, if you peanut butter and I'm jelly, then together we could make a tasty sandwich. Catch my drift?" The gang leader stopped talking and furled his brow. He leaned in close and whispered, though still loud enough for everyone to hear. "But if you not interested, then you ain't no use to me."

Goldie crushed the remaining half of the sandwich in his hand and oozed grape jelly onto the floor. The clumpy purple goo stained the bleached linoleum. His dark pupils zeroed in on Victor's eyes, and everyone else at the table directed their shadowy gazes at the skinny teacher in the baggy jumpsuit.

"We should leave now," James repeated, this time much louder.

Victor was unintimidated. He ignored Goldie's advances, shoveled a fork into whatever meat was on his food tray and piled it in his mouth without a care in the world. It tumbled down his throat and landed in his empty belly. He was hungry and hadn't eaten in days. Inhospitable dining companions wouldn't interfere with his meal. Like the white supremacists, the beady-eyed inmate with the gold tooth didn't faze Victor. They were all chess pieces in a dangerous game he had no interest in playing.

James now understood what God had meant when he said, "Protecting and guiding a soul until he fulfills his destiny." He'd hoped that rescuing Victor from the noose would have fulfilled his heavenly obligation, but that act of courage failed to release him from duty. This was going to be a long journey.

"Time to go," James said.

He yanked Victor by the collar and lifted him to a standing position. The sudden jolt startled everyone at the table, including Victor, who decided it was best to leave before any other unexpected bodily movements caused him trouble. The gang watched in silence as Victor stepped away from his food and shuffled across the cafeteria toward the exit. Because he'd lost so much weight, his pant legs covered his shoes and gave the illusion that he was gliding.

"Hey!" Goldie shouted. "Where are you going?"

Victor ignored him, but in the middle of his abrupt escape, he keeled over out of breath, put both hands on his knees and gasped for air.

"What are you doing?" James chided. "We have to keep going. We can't stop now."

He nudged Victor forward, but the former teacher wouldn't move. At first, James thought dehydration and weakness were causing the pain, but then he saw the hives spreading across Victor's body. They invaded his face, neck and arms. His skin turned crimson. His stomach rumbled in pain. Victor collapsed onto the floor and clutched his throat. Three orderlies ran over to help.

"Get him to the infirmary!" a guard yelled.

James bent down next to the collapsed inmate, unsure of what to do next. He felt a gnawing sensation in the pit of his stomach that he'd failed God.

An orderly put his mouth on Victor's and alternated between giving breaths and chest compressions. James contributed the only way he could. He prayed.

"I'm sorry I've let you down," he said in a murmur. "Don't let him die. Give me another chance."

CHAPTER 8
CONTRITION

The gentle voice cut through a haze of bright light and competed over the rattling of a cast-iron radiator. Hot water gushed through the pipes, which clanged like loose change in a washing machine.

"Can you hear me?"

The words came from a blurry silhouette backlit by sunshine pouring into the stale space through stained-glass windows. While he couldn't see the stranger's face, Victor was able to make out a white lab coat with the name *Jose* embroidered on the front pocket. There was also a vaulted, church-like ceiling.

"Are we in a holy place?" he mumbled, still not fully conscious.

James was wondering the same thing. He counted 14 stained-glass windows representing the Stations of the Cross. A kaleidoscope of colors depicted Jesus carrying his cross to an execution site atop a hill, soldiers nailing his arms into wooden beams and disciples putting his body in a tomb. Each image was more exquisite than the next.

"You're not in a church," the man said. "You're in the infirmary, which was once the prison chapel. The warden thought a medical unit was more practical than a prayer space."

The warden was also opposed to inmates worshiping a higher power, because in his mind, there was no greater power than himself. He controlled life and death within the prison's walls. He only allowed for the beautiful floor-to-ceiling windows because they were too expensive to replace. Otherwise, the Stations of the Cross would've been out along with the pews.

The stained-glass refracted the light and painted the sterile white floor a myriad of colors. Shades of purple, green, yellow, red and orange burst into the room.

"Lovely, isn't it," the orderly said.

Victor's vision was returning. He squinted to see the old man caring for him. His features remained fuzzy, except for grayish hair, wrinkled olive skin and light-blue eyes that sparkled like crystals.

"You're looking better," he said. "That's a good sign because we were worried about you. The doctor didn't think you'd pull through."

Victor gazed into the man's stark pupils and saw a benevolent energy rippling through a sea of sapphire. He felt a sublime calm and forgot about the lingering pain in his stomach and the splitting headache shooting from his forehead to his eyebrows.

"The medicine will make you groggy, but you'll feel better soon," the old man said.

"What... happened?" Victor asked.

The words slipped off his numb lips. His voice

was weak. His headache pounded his skull. James stood next to the IV drip, which was connected to a stringy vein in Victor's arm.

A muscular, stern-faced nurse wearing a matching white blouse and skirt shuffled papers at a small desk in the corner. She was the first woman James had seen within the prison's walls, but she was no ordinary woman. The nurse stood taller than most of the convicts, nearly as tall as Little Kip. Her legs were the size of tree trunks. Her biceps bulged from underneath her uniform. Every few minutes, she'd glanced at the ward's sole patient to see if he was still alive before returning to her dinner: a hamburger; cheese fries; and an extra-large strawberry milkshake. The nurse's chomping was louder than the clattering radiator.

"Her name is Betty," the orderly said. "She'll care for you when I'm not around. We're working to get the poison out of your system. Someone slipped arsenic into your food. The guards found it mixed in with your mashed potatoes. Did you taste anything strange?"

Victor shook his head no.

"Lucky for you, it wasn't a fatal dose, only enough to make you sick. You've been vomiting for the past hour. Do you know who would want to kill you?"

Victor shrugged. The truth was he had many enemies, and it was unclear to him as to why. He mostly kept to himself and only interacted with others when necessary. But in prison, trouble seemed to find him.

There was a litany of suspects, and it'd be near impossible to find the culprit because no one was willing to snitch to the guards. Someone must have snuck the poison into his food in the kitchen or at the table where he'd been eating. It could've been Goldie. His cafeteria harangue had distracted Victor from the gang-bangers surrounding him — it's possible one of his minions orchestrated the scheme — or it could have been Little Kip and the white supremacists; he anticipated a clandestine attack was on the horizon.

Victor ran through a mental check list of everyone he'd encountered in the dining hall but couldn't recall anyone tampering with his plate. It was plausible the assassin was part of the kitchen staff. A few bribes here. A few bribes there. Money made the world go 'round, especially in prison. Victor's adversaries could have recruited and paid off a server.

"This is my fault," James said, shaking his head. "I should've done more."

The orderly leaned in and put his face mere inches from his patient. When he smiled, the wrinkles underneath his eyes spread out like branches on a tree. The octogenarian shifted his weight onto a mahogany cane supporting a bum knee.

"Sometimes, we need eyes behind our heads, especially in *here*," he said. He pointed proudly to the embroidered letters on his coat. "My name is Jose."

James felt warmth emanating from the elderly inmate turned caretaker, who shuffled along the edge of Victor's bed, sidestepping the spirit guide. It was the first time anyone went out of their way to avoid physical contact with James. Jose could have passed through him without incident, but instead, chose to walk around.

Can he see me?

"Take these pills." Jose handed Victor a small

paper cup with pink capsules. "They'll make you feel better and will help with the pain."

After the ordeal in the cafeteria, Victor was skeptical of ingesting foreign objects given to him by strangers, but for some reason, he trusted the old man. The muscles in his throat burned as he swallowed the pills and forced them down with a glass of orange juice. They landed hard in his stomach.

"Your throat almost closed up," Jose said. "Thank God you survived."

"Thank God," Victor repeated with regret.

Yet another missed opportunity. Maybe the third time would be a charm.

"So, you're the former teacher who drove drunk?" the orderly asked.

Victor's face turned red. His infamy had preceded him. Everyone at Watermill was aware of his crime. There were no secrets in prison.

"Yup," he said and turned his head away.

"We all make decisions that affect our lives. I'm an old man still accounting for my sins. I've accepted my punishment. In here, we watch the clock tick away but that doesn't mean it's too late for redemption."

Victor was unsure how to respond.

"Why are you helping me?" he asked.

"Because we both need to forgive ourselves in order to move on. We still have a purpose in life, even in a place like this."

But how did I forgive? James wondered.

The spirit guide stared at the boney figure stretched out in the hospital bed and walked away in disgust. He looked toward the stained-glass window and saw a swaying forest on the other side of the security wall. The trees felt so close, he could smell the pine. Permafrost enveloped the auburn leaves. A red-tailed hawk swooped above a giant oak and glided down the valley. James wondered what else was beyond the tree line.

How long will I be stuck here? He asked himself.

"How long will I be here?" Victor asked Jose.

"You'll stay until you're healed. You need to rehabilitate your mind and body."

James was curious what his parents were doing. He wanted to meet his nephew and his brother's wife. They'd all looked happy at the picnic. He missed home and contemplated a great escape to visit his family. Was it wrong to leave Victor and violate his promise to God? So far, he was failing at being a protector.

"The pills are helping," Victor mumbled. "I'm feeling better."

A surge of energy reinvigorated his body. Blood flowed again and turned his pale cheeks a pinkish hue. His throat opened up. The searing pain in his skull subsided.

"You still have a lot of healing to do," Jose said. He felt Victor's forehead with his calloused hand. His body temperature had stabilized. "Forgiving yourself won't be easy. It's like hiking a mountain. There are dangerous rocks to scale, but once you reach the summit, you get a glimpse of heaven and realize it was all worth it."

For the briefest of moments, the orderly directed his penetrating gaze at James, who felt uneasy knowing his clandestine cloak may have been penetrated. Jose smirked and refocused his stare on the leafless tree branches bouncing in the frigid wind.

"What did you do to get sent to Watermill?" Victor asked, but Jose ignored his question.

"We never know when our end is near, so we must appreciate each day. We're all dealt a different hand, and we must play our cards the best we can. Victor, you and I played our hands poorly, but we can still make up for it."

Victor's eyelids drooped to a close, and for the first time in years, he fell into a dreamless slumber. No nightmares. No worries. No guilt. Only deep uninterrupted sleep.

"What we seek will come to us when we let it in," Jose said to the unconscious convict. His bright-blue marble eyes reflected the light. "Open your heart."

The old man limped toward a steel security door separating the infirmary from the rest of the prison. His hunch subtracted several inches from his diminutive frame.

"We have to take care of one another," he said as he walked away.

The nurse shot the elderly inmate a flippant glance and dismissed his rant as the musings of a time-worn convict. Jose used his cane to knock three times on the metal door. After a few seconds, an alarm buzzed, the bolts unlocked and two armed, uniformed guard appeared in the opening. A portly officer had an untucked shirt and food stains on his uniform. His skinny partner swam in an oversized jacket; a handgun in a leather holster on his belt weighed down his pants. Jose turned around and smiled in James's direction as the guards slammed the door shut.

*

The prison came alive at night. Doors creaked. Windows rattled. The wind howled through empty corridors. Inmates schemed in their cells. Whispers filled the darkness as deals were made and plans were hatched.

But some noises couldn't be so easily explained, like the chuckling from the laundry room in the basement, or the clicking of heels near the library entrance. During full moons, inmates claimed to see a woman with a lit candle walk through cell block 66. She never spoke and appeared to be in a hurry. Her apparition lingered for a few seconds before vanishing into a wall. It was unclear what or who she was looking for. Some believed she was the deceased mother of an inmate who'd come back to find her son.

At first, James was frightened by a wailing that echoed within the infirmary. He thought it one of the evil spirits roaming the prison, until he realized the weeping was coming from Victor's bed. The sounds of distress grew louder and spiraled into howls of anguish.

"I'm sorry!" Victor cried.

His grief thickened with every plea.

"I didn't mean to kill him. I didn't mean to hurt anyone."

He rolled out of his sheets, fell onto the linoleum floor and buried his face in his hands.

"I deserve to die!"

Every muscle in his body contorted. The gravity of his sins burdened his weakened soul and filled his heart with remorse.

"He didn't have to die. It should've been me. It's... all... my... fault."

Victor's cries went unanswered by the orderlies and became part of the sympathy of the night.

Tears streamed down James's cheeks. He put his arm around the inmate's boney shoulders. Victor was a weathered footnote of the past, a piece of gossip; a murmur in the halls of the school where he once taught: "Remember Mr. Young, who drove drunk and killed someone — whatever happened to him?"

Victor was unsure where the voice had come from, but he heard a whisper as faint as a feather floating in the breeze.

"I forgive you."

CHAPTER 9
WHAT HIDES IN THE SHADOWS

James was an innocent man trapped among criminals, and through Victor, he learned the ways of prison life, including the banal routines, listless guards, and tedious chores. Convicts serving the first year of their sentence despised the monotony. Some even went insane and succeeded where Victor had failed. Like a hamster on a wheel, they were all stuck in a perilous place.

In the annals of the correctional facility, there were several valiant attempts at escape, yet not a single inmate accomplished the feat. If the army of guards, the 25-foot tall concrete walls and the jungles of barbed wire weren't enough of a deterrent, Mother Nature proved more insurmountable. The prison was a citadel that sat atop a mountain overlooking an expansive valley near the border with Vermont. Natural wonders intersected with the depraved city on a hill. Moose, bear, mountain goats, coyote and bobcats roamed the pine forests and followed the river that passed through a portion of the penitentiary before cascading into a powerful waterfall. The water flowed adjacent to the penal farm and was off limits to most inmates, especially ones convicted of more serious crimes. Work assignments at the farm were given only to non-violent offenders with good behavior, which eliminated most of the prison population.

Many dreamt about making an aquatic escape by swimming downstream, but even if they managed to elude the armed guards stationed in the perimeter towers, they'd drown or freeze. At night, temperatures plunged below zero and forced even the animals to take shelter in the mountain's shadowy crevices.

One inmate who managed to get beyond the walls might have survived had he done the same. In 1990, 31-year-old Elias Seymore tunneled underneath the prison through the inner workings of its aging sewer system. While washing linens in the laundry room, he'd discovered an unused utility closet with an access door. The professional burglar easily picked the lock and found his path to freedom. Seymore used a power saw smuggled to him by a crooked guard to cut his way into one of the larger pipes. With darkness as his cover, he relied on a flashlight to guide him through a pipeline that emptied into the waterfall. Somehow, he survived the 50-foot drop but froze to death three miles from the prison. Bloodhounds led the guards to his body between two oak trees.

Each day at Watermill started with an early breakfast followed by a work assignment like cooking, landscaping or laundry. Depending on the season, one job might be better than another; laundry duty was ideal in the winter when the industrial dryers warmed the prison basement, but in the summer, the machines turned the cool cellar into a sweat factory. The same was true for outdoor work. Planting in the garden and raking leaves were better options than shoveling snow in frigid temperatures.

Lunch followed the monotonous chores. Creative cooks concocted sandwiches out of whatever they could slap on stale bread. If inmates were lucky, it might be ham and cheese, but more often than not, it was a mysterious meatloaf. Peanut butter and jelly was a safer bet, but not for Victor.

Free time followed lunch. Inmates roamed the exercise yard, where trouble brewed. Most of the gangs formed along racial lines. They'd cordon off territories and scheme out in the open. Even tables in the dining hall were designated for specific gangs. Each one functioned like a criminal enterprise. They used their connections on the outside to facilitate drug deals on the inside. Dry-cleaning loads and food-delivery pallets provided cover for trafficking marijuana, heroin and cocaine. A casual search by a guard with pockets bulging from bribe money was pure theatrics.

"Looks good," a corrections officer would shout and slap the side of a truck hauling the tainted cargo. As long as contraband wasn't falling out of boxes, it cleared inspection.

If you weren't in a gang, then you were a loner like Victor, and that was dangerous. Some loners were mentally ill and easy to spot. They were the ones kicking up dirt, mumbling prophesies and pointing at sparrows. The gang-bangers left them alone, and for that reason, Victor and James wondered if the *crazies* were indeed crazy at all. A handful put on a good show to avoid confrontation. They kept up the act throughout their sentences, which meant years of deception. Victor wondered if he too could fake insanity but decided against it because he was a terrible actor — so much for being an English teacher.

James pulverized a maple leaf between his thumb and index finger. Specks of red dust rained onto his feet. Most of the leaves had already fallen and all but a few had turned a rusty brown. They swirled into a harmonious cyclone. He sucked in the cool chill through his nostrils and let the cold air fill his lungs. Winter was around the corner. He could taste it.

"I enjoy when you get outdoor assignment on days like this," James said. "The foliage in the valley below must be beautiful. If only we could get beyond these walls for a peek."

Victor lifted his head from raking. He thought he heard a whisper, but it was probably a bird. He turned his attention back to clearing leaves. It'd been that way for more than a year, and James had come to accept his invisible role. He was an ineffable energy force in the background, guiding a man who remained ignorant to his presence. But while Victor couldn't hear the spirit guide's words, he was beginning to feel him in his heart.

"Lily and I loved apple-picking." The memory brought a smile to his face. "Sometimes, we'd skip class and go to the orchard. I'm sure you wouldn't approve of that as a teacher, but we'd have so much fun. She insisted on hauling a basket of apples that was bigger than her."

James broke into a laughing spell before continuing his story.

"One time, she tried carrying it up a hill but slipped and all of the apples rolled into the mud. It was both heartbreaking and hilarious. I never let her forget that day, and she hated me for it! The funny thing was that her favorite season was fall, but her favorite place was the beach. She was walking contradiction, but I loved her. I loved everything about her."

Victor ignored James and snatched a brittle leaf drifting through the air. It'd fallen from a sycamore, and despite the change in seasons, hadn't yet changed colors. Both sides were speckled lime green.

"Looks like you fell too soon," Victor said.

He tucked away the veiny leaf into the breast pocket of his jacket.

*

The lightbulbs lining the narrow hallway hissed at Victor and his spirit guide. The noise reminded James of the reptile house at the zoo. His mind wandered to Little Gerry, and he wondered what his snake was doing — maybe enjoying the beach with God or curling into a ball near the mangrove trees. If there was ever such thing as a gentle snake, Little Gerry was it. The ball python never bit any of James's friends. Like a purring cat, he'd press his body to the ground whenever someone stroked his scales.

The underground passage led from the shed near the river to the center of the prison; all of the buildings at Watermill were linked through a network of tunnels. Inmates used the secret passageways to move precious cargo, like drugs and contraband, without attracting the guards' attention. The walls were stone, except for several doors made of corroded-iron bars, remnants of old solitary-confinement cells now used for storage. James peered into one of the rooms but could only make out boxes and cobwebs.

He always sensed danger when walking through the tunnels, but on this trip his unease was deepened. A morose feeling filled his chest and spread down his legs. He'd experienced the same sensation in the cafeteria when Victor was poisoned. The spirit guide darted down the hallway to catch up with Victor, who'd gotten ahead. In the dim light, he saw the convict's skeletal silhouette as well as the shadows of four others who were surrounding him. He wondered how the men had snuck up on Victor without making any noise, seemingly appearing out of thin air. The troubled feeling lingered. When he reached the group, he found the warden and two guards on either side of an inmate in handcuffs.

"You're the former teacher," the warden said while adjusting the glasses resting on his beak-like nose. His lanky arms and legs gave the appearance of a flightless bird, which had earned him the nickname the Crane. Even the guards adopted the cruel moniker, behind his back of course; no one risked inciting his infamous temper.

"Victor Young, correct?" he asked.

"Yes, sir."

Warden Rufus Covington Hitchcock III was the scion of Boston Brahmins, who'd dominated the New England textile industry since the Industrial

Revolution. The Hitchcock's had owned a watermill and clothing factory overlooking a mountainous valley before they sold the property to the State of New York. Legislators dealing with a burgeoning prison population used the sale as an opportunity to expand the department of corrections. So, a watermill that once housed overworked, cheap labor became home to imprisoned labor. The deal included a cushy perch for the oldest son of the family to oversee the day-to-day operations of the penitentiary.

The Hitchcock family fortune ensured the Crane a lifetime of comfortable luxury, but power, not money, was what nourished his soul. His notorious rein at Watermill included removing mattresses from the cells of inmates who'd committed minor violations like sneaking beer into the exercise yard, to ordering the lobotomy of a severely schizophrenic prisoner. After the inmate attacked a prison guard with a fork, the Crane had enough. He filed the necessary paperwork to make the family-less man a ward of the state. From the warden's perspective, the lobotomy was a success. The inmate's bad behavior ended along with his ability to perform simple tasks like holding a spoon. The man lived out the rest of his days as a zombie. The procedure was a warning to all others: follow the rules or else.

Victor stood straight and pushed out his chest. The warden was taller but skinnier. A strong gust of wind might blow him over.

"We're escorting this man to the tombs for…" The warden paused to contemplate his phrasing. "Violations — several of them."

"The tombs" was prison slang for solitary confinement, located several levels underground and more dismal than the older holding cells they'd passed. Each tomb was without light, forcing the punished inmate to exist in utter darkness. Some communicated with their neighbors by tapping on the walls in code because talking was not allowed. The doors were made of solid steel, and the guards gave unlucky inhabitants meals through a mailbox-like opening. Rations were meager and inmates who didn't consume all of their food in one sitting discovered that the rats ate the leftovers. Depending on the offense, solitary confinement ranged from a few days to a few weeks.

Both James and Victor recognized the man in handcuffs bookended by the guards. He looked different from the last time they saw him in the cafeteria. His neatly-pressed jumpsuit was now wrinkled and stained by dirt following a beat down by a corrections officer in the mechanics shop. His ring was gone and so was the gold tooth with the diamond-lighting bolt. It had fallen out after a guard's sucker punch landed perfectly on his jaw. A gaping hole took its place. Winston Victorians, a.k.a Goldie, knew all of his attackers, including the one who'd hit him, but it'd do him more harm than good to blow the whistle.

When the warden asked, "Who did this to you?" Goldie knew the question was a trap. Hitchcock could care less about who roughed up the drug dealer from Brooklyn. He was more interested in coaxing Goldie into snitching because he knew the punishment behind closed doors would be more severe. The gang leader had gotten pinched for a narcotics shipment he'd arranged into the prison. When a guard who failed to receive his bribe payment uncovered the delivery, he blew the lid on the scheme.

"Mr. Victorians will spend a week in the tombs to think about what he did," the warden said. "His absence will leave an opening in the mechanics shop. Mr. Young, if you'd like a change of scenery, I'm more than happy to oblige a new work responsibility. I believe you're currently assigned to outdoor duty."

Victor was taken back by the offer. Winter was around the corner and working inside was appealing. There was only one small problem — he knew nothing about repairing cars and trucks. Plus, he had no desire to get behind the wheel of anything ever again. The idea of driving and potentially killing another person scared him. He felt that it was a privilege he'd deserved to lose.

"Maybe you should ask him about the library." James said. "It's better suited for your skill set."

"What about the library?" Victor blurted, surprised at his response. The idea had just come to him. He fumbled with a follow-up explanation. "Well... you see... I used to teach... and... um... I have... um... a passion... for books."

The warden arched his eyebrows. Victor prepared for a rebuke. Instead, Hitchcock paused for several seconds before curling a smile from underneath his beak-like nose.

"That could be arranged. I do have a need for someone to oversee the record room which is part of the library."

Without saying another word, the warden brushed past Victor and continued toward the tombs. The wooden heals of his dress shoes clicked against the concrete. The guards followed and dragged their moaning prisoner. Goldie's white sneakers scraped the ground as he was pulled deeper into the earth. Victor wondered if Goldie was responsible for trying to kill him in the cafeteria, but he'd come to accept he might never find out.

James and Victor walked in the opposite direction down the twisted, dark hallway toward their cell block. For the first time in years, Victor smiled. It was genuine and sincere. He'd found hope in books, and he had his favorites: *The Adventures of Sherlock Holmes*; *To Kill a Mockingbird*; *The Art of War*. He'd avoided the prison library because he lost his passion for everything, especially literature, but the prospect of being surrounded by something he loved sparked excitement in the defeated man. He thought of Plutarch: "The measure of a man is the way he bears up under misfortune." The former teacher might add, "Misfortune caused by his own doing."

Whatever crashed into his skull, hit him with such force, his body smashed into the stone wall and slid to the ground like a rain drop trickling down a window pane. His vision blurred. His brain bounced around his skull. The boot kick to his chest shattered a rib. Victor howled in pain. There was little fat on his belly to absorb the blows.

The skeleton covered in black ink hovered over him with a menacing glare. He flashed two sets of teeth — his real ones and the ones tattooed on his skin. Had the demons finally come to carry him? If so, he was ready.

"Not yet," a gruff voice mumbled from the shadows.

Little Kip's bald head inched into a sliver of light. A black eyepatch emerged, while the rest of his face remained shrouded in darkness.

"Me and Bones been hiding out in this cell waiting for you," he said. "We would've got you sooner if the warden didn't walk by."

The giant hacked up a ball of phlegm from deep within his chest and spat a wad of mucus that landed mere inches from Victor's head.

"How come you been ignoring me all this time? You thought I was going to forget about our conversation? Not me. I never forget nothing."

Victor had gone out of his way to avoid Little Kip and his acolytes following the cafeteria incident and had been successful — until now.

Bones stood adjacent to the boss and jostled back and forth in anticipation of violence, itching for the orders to destroy the skinny man reeling on the ground. Meanwhile, James stood beside Victor. The spirit guide was outnumbered two to one. His mind rushed into high gear as he contemplated a plan of attack. He had to do something. Otherwise, Victor would die. Little Kip stepped farther into the light to reveal the Confederate flag tattoo on his arm.

"I gave you a chance to join our cause, but you squandered it. You fraternized with the enemy and turned down my offer. Why openly disrespect the one person who could protect you?"

Victor peered up at his attackers and whispered what sounded like a prayer. Little Kip and Bones were taken back, unsure if their prey was conjuring some greater spirit to his rescue. James had noticed that Victor was praying every night following his stint in the infirmary. Nothing ritualistic. No signs of the

ANGELS ON THE BRIDGE

cross. Only whispers and phrases. Personal conversations with God while raking leaves, showering or even eating. Victor was never religious and rarely went to church, so James wondered if his own presence engendered this newfound spirituality blossoming in a place where little else did.

"I've been ignoring you..." Victor paused to spit out blood and a tooth, which tumbled along the ground until it reached Little Kip's feet. "...because I don't associate with ignorant bastards like yourself."

James's jaw dropped. So did Little Kip's. The bald behemoth lost his smirk and brushed back the skeleton to give himself enough space to finish the job. James knew if he didn't act fast, his friend would be pulverized.

The spirit guide used all of his strength to jump into the air and grab a water pipe fastened to the ceiling. His fingers warmed from the hot water flowing through the metal cylinder. He then pulled down on the pipe with all of his strength. The rattling startled the two assailants standing underneath it, and they stepped back as the rusted pipe bounced above their heads. James tried to dislodge the piping with the hopes of sending scalding water toward the attackers, but the spirit guide was distracted by noises coming from the shadows — a crunch of breaking bones followed by a scream.

"My eye!" Little Kip yelled. "I can't see nothing!"

The gang leader stumbled to the ground and landed next to Victor. He pressed his hands to his good eye, the one without the patch. In-between the shrieking, James heard wood splintering, followed by Bones dropping to the ground and landing on top of Little Kip.

"Get off me, you idiot! I can't see!"

But Bones was lifeless. His eyes had rolled into his head. A gash stretched across his forehead.

"Are you okay?" James asked Victor. He dropped from the pipe and rushed over to his side.

"These troublemakers got what they deserve," a familiar voice said. "They'll be fine. I gather they've had worse beatings than one from an old man."

Jose limped out of the holding cell with a splintered cane in tow. The 80-year-old was less steady without his wooden support. All that was left was a curved handle jutting to a spike.

Little Kip moaned on the ground.

"You're lucky I didn't stab you," Jose barked. "Don't worry — you'll be able to see again. The blindness is temporary."

James's eyes widened. Somehow, the elderly inmate with arthritis and a crooked spine had used ninja-like skills to take out two of Watermill's most dangerous residents.

"How did you do that?" the spirit guide asked.

"I was coming from the infirmary when I saw these two goons sneak down the hallway. I had a feeling they were up to no good, so I followed them. My cane was the secret weapon." He waved the broken wood in the air. "At least, what's left of it."

Jose helped Victor to his feet. His legs were wobbly, and he grabbed onto the old man's shoulder for support.

"Thank you," Victor said.

The distant sound of wooden heals got louder as the warden came into view. He raced down the hallway with two guards who had their guns drawn. They stopped short when they came upon the unusual scene: one of the oldest inmates at Watermill, accompanied by the skinniest and arguably the weakest, stood over the bodies of the notorious white supremacists.

"Well, shit," Hitchcock said as he scratched his head.

"Warden, I'll take the blame for this one," Jose said with confidence. "These two knuckleheads attacked this fella. I saw it happen, and luckily for... what did you say your name was again, son?"

"Victor."

"Yes...luckily for Victor, I jumped in to help. All it took was some whacks to the head, and they fell down like lead. If you ask me, they needed to learn a lesson."

The warden cocked his head at the elderly convict and shot him an expressionless stare before breaking into a smile.

"Mr. Martinez, I don't know how you accomplished what I've only dreamed of doing since my first day on the job. You should get a medal."

Hitchcock turned to his guards.

"Carry these bastards to the infirmary, and when you're done, give the old man a steak dinner. Martinez — go to the hospital ward and make sure they don't die. When you're done, you'll get your supper."

"Yes sir," Jose and the guards said in unison.

The uniformed officers dragged the injured inmates by their arms to the hospital wing and disappeared down the hallway. The warden exited down a separate corridor without saying another word.

James had a strange feeling that it'd be the last time he see Little Kip, and he was right. The strongman was transferred to a medical facility in Western New York for ophthalmological treatment. His vision did return, like Jose had promised, but not fully. He lived a blurry existence for the remainder of his days, and the world was safer because of it.

"How were you able to beat them back with a cane?" Victor asked his fragile-looking friend.

"Luck and prayer."

CHAPTER 10
IT'S NOT YOUR TIME

The combined euphoric odor of fresh plastic, vinyl and stitched leather tickled Victor's nostrils. He slid into the bucket seat. A wave of excitement built in his chest. He shut the door to the sparkling, fire-engine red Corvette and gripped the steering wheel like a bull rider grabbing the wrap. It was time to unleash the beast.

But there was something unusual about his hands. They were wrinkly and blotchy. He adjusted the rearview mirror and glanced at his reflection. The hazel pupils staring back at him were the same, but the skin around his eyes was drooping. His forehead creased and folded in flaps. His skin was blemished with moles and dark spots.

"Are you going to drive or stare at yourself all day?" a young man in the passenger seat asked.

A baseball cap cast a shadow over his face. Aviator sunglasses shielded his eyes. While he couldn't make out the man's features, Victor knew who he was and had feared this moment in his nightmares. He envisioned their encounter would be filled with rage; the animosity was well-deserved, and Victor deserved no pity.

But instead of ferocious reciprocity, James St. George emanated kindness. The amicable energy surprised Victor, who questioned whether their interaction was a trick. He wanted to apologize for what he'd done, but before he could speak, James interrupted, "This is not a trick, so are you going to start this thing and drive or waste more precious time?"

Victor turned the key, and the 500-horsepower engine roared to life. He pressed his foot to the gas, and the engine growled back in a cacophony of belts and pistons working in unison. The speedometer spiked higher and higher — 6,000 RPM's, 7,000 RPM's, 8,000 RPM's. The mechanical orchestra awaited direction from its conductor, and when the tachometer crested above the 9,000 mark, Victor set the tempo to full speed ahead.

The tires screeched and spun in place. Rubber seared the blacktop. White smoke shot in the sky. The stench of burning replaced that new-car smell, still no less pleasing to the senses. For the briefest of moments, the fiery convertible hovered from left to right before bolting forward.

Centripetal force shot Victor deeper into his seat. He already felt as if he was sitting on the ground, but now he was nearly parallel to the road. With both hands glued to the steering wheel, he struggled to maintain control of the beautiful machine and used all his strength to guide the Corvette around the twisting turns cutting through the hills. The car's extra-wide chassis hugged the pavement. Their bodies shifted with every sharp curve.

They flew underneath a canopy of tree branches and flashed down a rural stretch. A flock of sheep watched the red rocket from an open field filled with daisies, violets, and poppies. But there was no time to savor the bucolic sights. Victor shifted into fifth gear, and the scenery became a blur of shapes and colors. The wind stung his eyes and ripped back his thinning hair. He wiped away the tears and smirked. His dimples deepened. James was smiling too. Their laughter echoed high above the engine's roar.

"What do the vibrations feel like in the shifter?" James shouted over the wind.

"Amazing!" Victor yelled while barreling into a turn. The whistling breeze drowned out much of his voice. "She handles great!" He shifted into sixth gear. "Nothing like I've ever driven." He downshifted. "So fast!"

Unlike Victor, James hadn't aged. His muscular arms bulged from his white T-shirt. His skin was smooth, tan and wrinkle-free. With the car flying at full speed, he forced out his shaky hand to give Victor a thumbs-up.

"Guide her, and she'll do all the work," he shouted over the rattling. "Hit the gas hard when you take the turn."

Victor laughed with excitement and fell into a coughing spell. His aging body could only handle so much.

The two spoke little during their race through the countryside, but their expressions said it all. The older pilot and his younger companion savored the roller coaster ride. Their journey took them along

cliffs suspended above a roaring ocean. Waves
crashed against jagged rocks. The blacktop spiraled
down to a beach filled with soft, powdery, pinkish
sand. A giant turtle lying in the simmering heat
watched the speeding convertible shoot through a
cloud of dust. They sped into an auburn desert
replete with Joshua trees and prickly cactuses. The
dunes were as tall as mountains. A red-rock
formation climbed out of the earth and surrounded a
sparkling waterfall that emptied into a winding
stream. A cluster of lizards scurried along the water's
edge. Then, they sailed through a wintery forest
where the pine needles were encased in ice. Snowy
owls swooped above the car. Their cheeks, sweaty
from the desert, turned cold in the frigid air, and they
could see their smoky breath. Silver dollar snowflakes
melted on their faces. The Corvette slid across a
frozen lake. Victor peered over the driver's side door
and saw a school of trout swimming underneath the
convertible. The tires spun without traction as the car
glided toward a green meadow filled with sunflowers.
They followed a gravel road on the other side of the
lake to a stone building with a copper roof. The sun's
rays reflected off its shiny metal and forced James to
readjust his sunglasses. Two oak doors with purple
fleur-de-lis stained-glass windows marked the
entrance. Rounded shrubs and hydrangeas encircled
the rectangular building made of limestone and
granite.

"This is where I used to teach," Victor announced
with pride. He parked the convertible in front of the
school and shut off the engine. It hissed to a rest.
Icicles melted on the front grill. Two soccer goals
with fresh coats of white paint sat on either end of an

empty field next to the school.

"I coached soccer every day after class," Victor said as he and James sauntered toward the practice field. "We had an amazing team. Our strikers were quick, and our backline was strong. Like they say, 'Offense wins games, but defense wins championships.' No one expected us to win much of anything, but can you believe that we made it all the way to the state championship and won! What a season. I'll never forget it. The principal put the trophy in the lobby for everyone to see. I like to think my coaching had something to do with the victory, but the truth is that the players were amazing."

The grounds were impeccably kept. The sweet air smelled of freshly-cut grass.

"This is where I was happiest in my life. It's where I fell in love and met my wife."

Victor paused and stared at James with curiosity.

"Is she here now?"

James shook his head.

"That's okay." Victor said and stared at his feet in disappointment. "I was hoping to see her, but another time."

They walked passed a wooden bench underneath a willow tree that climbed high above the school.

"It took my students in shop class an entire semester to build that bench, and as you can see, it's stood the test of time."

Victor climbed the brick steps at the entrance and grabbed the brass-door handles in the shape of roaring lions (the school's mascot), but when he tried to open the doors, James put his hand on his shoulder and pulled down his arm. The old man raised his gray eyebrows in confusion.

"I want to go inside to show you the school. The architecture is amazing, and there are views of rolling mountains from every room. You also have to see the state championship trophy that I was telling you about. It's spectacular silver cup and all of our names are engraved in the base."

"I want to see all of those things, but not yet," James said.

"Why not?"

"We have to go back."

The elderly man squared his body to James in defiance.

"I don't want to go back. Why would I want to leave such a beautiful place? This is where I should stay."

James put his hand on Victor's shoulder and squeezed.

"You can't stay. It's not your time."

CHAPTER 11
THE SECRET ROOM

Victor exhaled into his palms and rubbed them together inches from his nose. The radiator in the library was broken, and no one had come to fix it. It'd been that way for several weeks. He knew he'd need to bribe one of the plumbers with cash to get the job done, cash he didn't have in his dwindling commissary account.

"We've got more pressing needs in the dead of winter than repairing pipes in a room that nobody uses," the building supervisor told him.

"Since when is heat not a pressing need?" a defeated Victor pleaded. So, jackets, hats and scarves became the apparel of choice for any inmate perusing the stacks of the Watermill Correctional Facility library for a good read on a frigid day.

The warden stuck to his word and gave Victor the post of librarian and record keeper. There wasn't much competition for the job. Not many inmates were lining up to manage a room filled with dusty books. Still, Victor loved the work. He organized the cavernous space, which was being used mostly for storage. Boxes stuffed with records were stacked floor to ceiling. Paperbacks and hardcovers were separated, but there was otherwise no discernible order. It was impossible to find anything in the hodgepodge. Genres were mixed together, and nothing was alphabetized.

"Science fiction, non-fiction, poetry, biography," Victor mumbled to himself as he shuffled through books like a deck of cards. His immediate goal was to categorize the collection. Maybe a functional library would encourage more inmates to read. He felt as though he was back in school, but instead of teaching adolescents, he was trying to motivate criminals.

"Ah, *Julius Caesar*," James said and pointed to a copy of the play resting atop a handyman's book on electrical wiring. "This was one of Lily's favorites. 'Cowards die many times before their deaths; the valiant never taste of death but once.' We read it in that damn literature course she forced me to take."

Victor flipped through one of the thicker texts on his desk and shook his head in disgust.

"You've got to be kidding me."

The pages in-between the leather binding of *War and Peace* had been hollowed to conceal contraband. The drug baggies were gone, but leftover white residue lingered on the pages.

"At least they didn't desecrate *20,000 Leagues Under the Sea*," Victor said. He inspected the novel's pages. Other than a ripped cover, it was in good shape. He picked up a roll of tape and scissors from his desk and worked to surgically repair the damage.

James was proud of Victor. The library was

coming together, and while there weren't many visitors, it was a respectable space. The former teacher had created order amidst chaos and found solace among books like Marcus Aurelius's *Meditations*, burying himself in the musings of the famous Roman emperor: "An end to your time here has been marked out, and if you do not use this time for clearing the clouds from your mind, it will be gone, and so will you."

After reading for several uninterrupted minutes, Victor drifted into a deep sleep but was awoken by a knock on the library door. James shifted uncomfortably in his chair. No one ever knocked. They just walked in. The silhouette in the door's cloudy glass pane was blurry.

"Come in," Victor said with the confidence of a supervisor beckoning a subordinate; even he was taken back by his tone.

The man who entered the room was over 6 feet tall and had a pot belly that poked out from his unbuttoned blazer. A skinny black tie rested on top of his large stomach. Gelled-down hair was parted in the middle. A bushy-black mustache hovered above his upper lip.

"I need a file," the stranger said without making any formal introduction. He avoided direct eye contact with Victor, and his gaze veered off to the side. He stuck his nose in the air as if he'd smelled something unpleasant.

"I'm more than happy to assist," Victor said. "May I ask who you are, and what your relationship is to the warden?"

Unlike his fellow inmates, Victor never cowered before authority. The worst they could do was send him to the tombs for insubordination, and in some ways, he welcomed solitary confinement as a respite from the madness.

"I am one of the superintendents, and that's all you need to know," he said pompously. The stranger combed his fingers through his mustache. "I need you to retrieve a file on an inmate named Harvey Lotion. When you locate this prisoner's file, please bring it to the warden's office."

His instructions were succinct yet unusual — why did he want the records of an inmate executed decades ago?

"I'm more than happy to search for his records, but it will take some time to..."

"Finding this file is your new priority," the superintendent snipped.

Without saying another world, the tall, heavy-set man spun around like a top and exited the library as quickly as he'd appeared, disappearing behind the frosty glass.

"What was that all about?" James asked. "He was one of the oddest people we've met in this place, and we've met some odd folks."

But Victor was more interested in why the warden and the other suits were interested in Harry Lotion, the last man executed at Watermill. A jury convicted the Bronx native of killing a father, his 12-year-old daughter and a cashier during a botched bodega robbery. After shooting the clerk in the chest, Lotion jumped behind the counter to clear the register of $320 but realized he wasn't alone in the shop. A man and a young girl were hiding in an aisle near the canned goods. Lotion fired at close range and killed them both. Unfortunately for the gunman, he bumped into responding officers while leaving the shop and emptied his chamber at the cops, shooting one in the shoulder before running out of bullets. He was corned in an alley, where he was tackled and handcuffed.

"I'm not gonna lie about what I did," Lotion told the judge in court. "I killed them two people. I probably wouldn't do nothing differently. My only regret is getting caught." He laughed out loud when he was sentenced to death.

Victor doubted Lotion's records were in the newer boxes mixed in with book drive donations from a local Boy Scouts troop — if only the eager scouts knew their books would go unread by the convicts on the hill. It was more likely the files were buried in the storage space underneath the library. The area was filled with a myriad of crumbling cardboard boxes that disintegrated when opened.

"Happy digging," James said. "You'll need a mask if you're going to rummage through the dusty mountains of documents."

A spiral staircase at the back of the library led to a shadowy room that housed old books, outdated texts and deteriorating records, including inmate files dating back to the prison's inception. A single switch controlled a series of naked lightbulbs dangling from wires connected to a low ceiling. Victor ducked to avoid smacking his head against support beams.

"The exposed wiring looks dangerous," James said. "I doubt the warden ordered a fire inspection. He'd rather have the whole building burn down with everyone in it than waste time on inspections."

Victor rummaged through the boxes while covering his mouth and nose with a white handkerchief. Cardboard disintegrated in his fingers, and the particles filtered into the air. One carton was stuffed with old newspaper. He felt the inky paper in-between his fingers and read the news with curiosity. A front-page story written July 8, 1987, was about the Iran-Contra deal and government officials testifying before Congress. Another story included a photograph from Spain of an American paratrooper being gored during the running of the bulls.

Victor coughed loudly. The less time he spent underneath the library the better; he needed to refocus on the task at hand. He thought of what the warden told him when he started the job, "You might come across interesting tidbits here or there amongst the records, but it's best you keep whatever you read to yourself. No need to spread gossip and cause a stir because you never know who you could upset. You could be putting yourself in jeopardy."

The threat was clear — he promised not to discuss anything he uncovered.

Despite hours combing through countless files and boxes, Victor was unsuccessful in finding the missing records. His cough was worsening too. The damp, dusty room clogged his lungs, and he wouldn't be able to spend much more time in the cramped space.

"If you stay down here any longer, you'll end up in the infirmary," James said.

Victor's arms shook from exhaustion. His eyes watered. He was about to give up when he noticed a pyramid of dilapidated boxes stacked in the shadows against a corner wall. He never noticed them before and decided to explore the contents before calling it a night. He'd already missed dinner, but the guards wouldn't make a fuss as long as he was back in his cell for the evening count.

He unstacked the crumbling cardboard boxes and found something he hadn't expected — a warped door. It had a circular hole where a knob was supposed to be. Victor carefully stuck his fingers into the dark space and prayed that nothing would grab him on the other side.

"Let's see where this thing leads," Victor said. "Maybe it's a secret way out of this place."

"One could only hope," James added.

Ever so gently, he pulled open the door, which was barely connected to the hinges. Its creaking sounded like a wailing banshee. The pungent air smacked them in the face. Victor covered his nose and mouth, and James rubbed away the chill crawling down his arms. The clandestine, windowless room was a perfect square — 20 feet by 20 feet — and was filled with more boxes.

The previous inmate in charge of the library had failed to mention this secret space, most likely because he'd forgotten about it. Victor had taken over from a 90-year-old with early-onset dementia. The old man's memory had gotten so bad, he'd forgotten how to walk back to his cell. Jose cared for him in the infirmary until he was transferred to a medical facility.

"X marks the spot," James said.

He pointed to a box deep within the clutter marked *Death Row* in red lettering. Victor saw it too and removed the top to examine manila envelopes stuffed inside, each stamped with a date representing a life extinguished behind bars. There was Harvey Goldberg, a financial accountant whose evening hobby was seducing young men and luring them back to his suburban home, where he murdered and butchered his dates — not necessarily in that order. There was Tommy Smith, a homeless man with a penchant for pushing straphangers in front of oncoming subway cars. Omar Winney raped and killed more than a dozen prostitutes. Nurse Cecil Smith poisoned his patients. And then, there was Harvey Lotion. Victor found his file at the top of the pack of Watermill's most notorious residents. He removed it without reading the contents. His job was done. Plus, he could care less about the details. He was more interested in the room.

*

Victor and James knelt down for what had become their afternoon ritual. The rickety floorboards squeaked underneath their weight. The altar before them was nothing more than a weathered cedar table pushed against the wall, courtesy of the shoddy carpenters in the woodworking shop. Victor thought his former high school students could've done a better job, but then again, having something was better than nothing. James also eyed the table with disgust and thought it an insult to the art of woodworking. He would've built the altar using hickory, the hardest of hardwoods, and envisioned attaching decorative carvings to the joints. He missed the carpentry shop.

Two tall candles with flickering flames and circular bases bookended a crooked cross. Victor had paid a smuggler in an adjacent cell block to procure the items. It cost him $35 which he thought was pricey, but the smuggler added a markup for the cross because it was considered risky contraband. The warden disdained religion. Punishment for sneaking in rosary beads or a Bible could be a week in the tombs.

Aside from the rickety table, two metal folding chairs and a standing lamp he borrowed from the library, the secret room was otherwise empty. No one bothered to ask Victor what he was up to because the library rarely had visitors. Occasionally, a few of the older convicts would wander in, grab a book and fall asleep on one of the worn leather couches. Victor had spent weeks clearing the room of boxes, folders stuffed with papers, a dozen dead mice, a tattered mattress, three unloaded rifles and containers holding the personal effects of inmates buried in the penal cemetery. With no family to claim their belongings, their clothes and keepsakes sat forgotten. In a box marked with the name *Valentine,* Victor found a pocket knife with the letter V carved into the handle. It was against code to possess any item deemed a weapon, such as a pocket knife, but he decided to keep it. Following the attack in the tunnel, he couldn't be too careful. Plus, the guards had stopped searching him since he became librarian.

James saw how the space became an escape for Victor, a refuge from a world of noise, a place for prayer and quiet reflection. Also, cleaning the secret room kept his mind occupied as the torpors of prison life dulled the senses and dampened the spirit.

"Weeping may endure for a night, but joy cometh in the morning," Victor whispered.

James was impressed with how the former teacher could recite countless verses from the Book of Psalms. Over the years, Victor had forgotten much

of what he'd learned in catholic school. The nuns
had forced him to read the Bible, but he never paid
much attention. Despite his limited knowledge of the
Old and New Testaments, he still remembered a few
verses from his altar boy days. So did James.

"Trust in the Lord with all your heart and lean not
upon your own understanding," the spirit guide said.

His mother had taught him that passage when he
was a boy. Every night before he went to sleep, she
knelt down next to the bed and prayed with him. He
could still hear her voice as he spoke the words, "In
all your ways acknowledge Him, and He shall direct
your paths."

Three quick knocks on the wooden door startled
both men, who whipped their heads around toward
the back of the room, but the excitement was short-
lived. They remembered that was the code.

"May I come in?" Jose asked.

"Of course," a relieved Victor said. "You scared
me. I thought you were the warden or one of his
henchmen."

"The warden and the guards don't knock. They
break down the door."

Jose was the only other person in the prison aware
of the secret room; Victor entrusted the old man with
his discovery. Whenever the infirmary got quiet, Jose
snuck into the library and shuffled down the metal
spiral staircase to pray in the de-facto chapel. Like
Victor, no one ever noticed whenever the elderly
inmate with the cane went missing.

"If we don't understand our lessons in life, then
we'll be forced to re-learn them in death," Jose said.
"The learning never stops. We must master patience
and compassion."

James thought Jose's message sounded familiar to what God had told him on the beach.

"How's the infirmary?" Victor asked.

"Ginger from cell block 10 got into an argument with his roommate over an unpaid bet. Both men pack a mean punch, but Ginger lost the bout and ended up with a concussion. The nurses are caring for him as we speak."

The old man settled into the squeaky chair and closed his eyes before falling into a deep slumber. James had never seen someone fall asleep so quickly.

"I guess you get tired faster when you're old," James said. "Good thing that I'm forever young."

The spirit guide smiled at his own joke.

Victor returned to his knees for prayer, but instead of reciting verse, he prayed.

"I'm sorry for what I've done. I'm sorry for hurting James."

James was taken aback. It was the first time he'd ever heard Victor mention him. During daily prayer, the former teacher begged God for forgiveness and expressed remorse for "killing that boy" but never spoke his name.

Victor reached into his pants pocket and pulled out a handwritten note on yellow legal paper along with a faded black-and-white photo of a young man. Much of the ink on the picture had smeared, but James was still able to make out the face in the 3 by 3 inch clipping. It had torn edges from where it'd been ripped out of a newspaper.

When the photographer snapped the portrait shot freshman year of college, James knew it'd be one for the ages, and not in a good way. His wrinkled gingham shirt and plaid tie were mismatched, the collar was two sizes too big and his dirty-blond hair was sticking out in every direction. He'd tried a new styling gel and wasn't pleased with the results — why he chose picture day to try a new hair product, he'd never know. The bottle went into the trash after he saw the photo, but there was no time to retake another before the start of school.

That image of an awkward 18-year-old kid embarrassed James both in life and death. When the school posted a picture board of incoming students in the main hall, James's clumsy grin was front and center. When he used his ID card to enter buildings on campus, his uncomfortable smile flashed on guards' computer screens. When a car piloted by a drunk driver killed him on the old stone bridge, it graced the front page of the local newspaper with the headline:

UNIVERSITY ALUM KILLED ON BRIDGE: Drunk Driver Arrested.

Victor's eyes scanned the yellow paper. His lips moved but he didn't speak the written words, so James peered over his shoulder to get a closer look at the letter.

Dear Mr. and Mrs. St. George,

There are no words to describe your pain. I can only imagine the shock you felt the day the police called you in the middle of the night.

To know that I'm the cause of that hollowness

brings me indescribable sorrow. Most days I wish I was dead. I even tried to kill myself but was unsuccessful... if only the noose had been stronger.

My prison sentence isn't a sufficient punishment for my crime. I've come to accept my doomed, eternal fate and the price I must pay for my sins. I wish I could go back and convince the stupid man driving that car to make a better decision.

I lost everything that night: my dignity; my freedom; my family; and most importantly, your son. I'm a character in a tragic tale of my own creation.

From the bottom of my heart, I'm sorry.

Sincerely,
Victor Young

The letter was dated a decade ago. Victor folded the crinkled parchment back into a stamped envelope. "Return to Sender" was written in red ink in his mother's handwriting above the delivery address.

CHAPTER 12
SELF-RELIANCE

The water from the rusted faucet cooled his sweaty face. Victor cupped the dribbling stream and splashed his cheeks and eyes. His heartbeat slowed. He took a deep breath.

Yet another dream — this one felt more real than the last.

He and James were stranded on a row-boat in the middle of the sea. They had only two oars, an 8-foot rope and a Swiss army knife. Land was nowhere in sight.

Despite their grim outlook, both men remained calm and even laughed together like two old friends who'd known each other for years. Victor talked about his favorite book, *The Great Gatsby*, and how it'd inspired him to become a teacher. James told him about the oak bookcase he was building for a pastor. Bulbous clouds in the shapes of animals hovered above their little boat and cast shadows on the water: a sea turtle; a snake; a stingray.

"Where are we going?" Victor asked.

"I don't know. The sea is carrying us."

"Do you think someone will rescue us?"

"I think we'll float to where we're supposed to be."

When they got thirsty, it rained. When they got hungry, fish jumped into the boat. Undulating waves carried them up and down in rhythmic motion, which made Victor sleepy. For the first time in years, he experienced pure, unadulterated happiness. He closed his eyes and fell asleep only to awake in his prison cell.

Prisoner #1030 gazed at the forlorn face staring back at him in the cracked mirror cemented to the wall. Over the years, he'd unsuccessfully tried to pry the glass loose, and once even punched it with his fist out of frustration. He'd found his reflection shameful, but as his soul healed, he learned to live with what he saw, even if he didn't like it.

While he hadn't yet aged like the older version of himself driving the sports car in his dreams, Victor thought his face looked weathered. Wrinkles surrounded his eyes. His hair had thinned. His cheek bones protruded through jaundiced skin. He moved more slowly because his joints ached. He wondered if he'd survive his sentence or die alone in prison.

If that's my fate, then so be it.

"Someone's coming," James said.

The rubber soles of the guard's boots squeaked against the concrete. The out-of-breath officer wearing an oversized uniform grabbed the bars of Victor's cell and clutched his chest. The young guard, who looked no older than 18 years, swallowed gulps of air before he managed to speak.

"He... told me... tell you..."

The teen pulled up his falling trousers but was losing to gravity. A baton and a flashlight weighed down his pants. A ring of keys clipped to his pocket clanged together as he unlocked the cell door and stepped inside.

"Infirmary... he..." Another breath followed more panting. "You should... go... see him."

"Slow down, fella," Victor said to his visitor. "Take a seat and catch your breath."

The young guard followed the prisoner's instructions, a first for Victor.

"What's happened in the infirmary?" James asked.

The guard waved his hand to signal he was about to speak but instead wiped beads of sweat from his brow.

"Take your time," Victor said. "You're not wasting mine, because I've got plenty to spare."

"It's your... orderly friend... Jose," the panting guard said. "You... have to... "

Victor stood up from his desk chair and put his hand on the guard's shoulder. Touching uniformed officers, however innocuous the gesture, was a violation at Watermill, but Victor didn't care. He needed to see his friend.

"Take me to him now," he demanded.

The guard nodded and led him out of the cell and down the hallway. Victor walked through the prison without handcuffs, a privilege he'd earned because of good behavior. With Little Kip nearly blind and living in a medical facility, Goldie in the crosshairs of the warden, and work responsibilities at the library, he could roam without fear of being attacked. He even felt an invisible force protecting him. The guards and other prisoners sensed it too. So, the bullying and abuse ended.

"We're almost there, but we have to move faster," James said.

Their pace quickened to a near jog. The young, skinny guard kept one hand on his utility belt to keep his pants from falling down. His untied boots nearly fell off. When they reached the infirmary, the trio found Jose alone in a bed near a stained-glass window. Sunlight reflected magenta and turquoise onto his white blanket. He was the only patient in the ward. His cheeks had lost their pinkish hue. His skin was droopy and cold. The simplest of movements required great energy. He labored to blink.

"Hi," he squeaked out in a weak voice. "Did you read the essay?"

After learning the crash that killed James happened in a town named after Ralph Waldo Emerson, the great American author who led the Transcendentalist Movement, Jose had recommended Victor read *Self-Reliance*. As the elderly orderly explained, Emerson espoused the creative spirit of the individual and subscribed to the idea that people and nature were inherently good. Transcendentalists believed all individuals possessed a piece of God, which united mankind.

Victor shook his head in disappointment. He'd devoured Emerson's works, and also read Whitman and Thoreau, but had failed to find a copy of *Self-Reliance*. It was missing from the prison library.

"I searched everywhere but came up empty," he said. "I promise I'll get my hands on a copy."

Jose forced out a grin and winced in pain.

"I wonder if one of the great thinkers in our concrete jungle is devouring it," the orderly said.

"One can only hope."

James put his hand on Jose's chest to feel his slowing heart. The spirit guide sensed that death was near. Still, Jose had a shimmer of life in his crystal-blue eyes.

"Did you come to say goodbye?"

"We came to make sure you're okay," James said.

"I'm holding up the best I can. Can I have something for the pain?"

The young guard walked over to the nurse in the white uniform who was chomping down on French fries at her desk. The request for pain pills got sidetracked in a conversation over food.

"Don't give up now," Victor pleaded to his friend. "You'll be better soon."

"They're all waiting for me," Jose said, closing his eyes. "They've been waiting for some time."

"Who's waiting for you?" Victor asked, his eyes widened with curiosity.

Jose ignored him.

"Death is cleansing." Another deep breath. "My soul is ready."

"You can't go." Victor fell onto his knees next to the hospital bed and leaned in toward the sick orderly. "You're all I've got. I don't know what I'd do without you."

"That's not true," Jose shot back, but his excitement proved too much for his failing body. He gasped for air and grabbed onto the side railings of his hospital bed. His forearms were bruised from the many jabbing attempts by nurses looking for usable veins.

"Your spirit guide will carry you forward."

Jose looked at James, who took two clumsy steps

backwards.

"Spirit guide?" Victor asked.

"Ask for help whenever you need it, and he'll be there. You're never alone when you have hope."

The old man swallowed hard. Sores had consumed his esophagus.

"Who is my spirit guide?"

"You'll meet him when you're ready"

"Will I see you on the other side?"

Jose nodded.

"I'll be there waiting for you," the orderly said.

Victor and James watched Jose's pupils morph from an ocean blue to a rich emerald before dissolving into a rusty auburn. The old man shut his eyelids one final time, and the kaleidoscope of colors vanished. The muscles in his body went limp.

A field of energy filled the infirmary, and the overhead lights brightened for a split second before dimming back to normal. The spirit guide felt an electric shock on his neck which ran down his back and into his legs before fizzling in his feet.

Victor put his hand on Jose's cold forehead. His only friend, the only person who'd ever showed him kindness following the crash, was gone. Yet again, he felt alone.

James wrapped his arm around Victor's shoulders and was surprised to feel other hands doing the same. Their fingers interlocked and formed a protective barrier around the mourning inmate.

CHAPTER 13
THREE MEN IN SUITS

The warm wind snuck in through an open window and filled the musty room with a sweet scent. James admired the portraits of wardens past in the wood-paneled room decorated with cherry molding. Each bearded face hung in a gold frame. The inscriptions beneath the paintings included years of service along with stuffy names like Sullivan Conwell III, Seamus Winston and Harley Humphrey. They were the lords of a fiefdom filled with criminals. Rufus Covington Hitchcock III would soon have his own portrait too, but he'd have to compete for real estate on the wall because there was little remaining space.

"I've got a feeling one of these dead guys will get bumped to the library when it's time to hang the Crane's portrait," James said.

Most inmates shuddered when they heard the clicking of the warden's dress shoes. He only made appearances when something was wrong, which more often than not meant that someone was going to be punished. For the most part, the warden left the prison librarian alone, except when he needed records.

"Maybe he'll remove all of the paintings to make room for his own," James said, brushing his finger along one of the gilded frames. "He wouldn't want to take away from his own glory."

Opposite Victor at the end of a rectangular mahogany table sat three men in suits drinking black tea. None offered any to Victor.

"It looks like our friend the superintendent is back, but I don't recognize the man to the warden's left," the spirit guide said.

The superintendent held the ceramic handle of his cup with his thumb and index finger and stuck out his pinky at a slight angle. His large gut resting on the edge of the table was disproportionate to the rest of his body: pencil-thin neck; thick mustache; elongated face. A few strands of hair broke free from the globs of gel holding down his perfect part and swayed with the breeze coming from the window. Like the last time they saw him in the library, he refused to look directly at the inmate sitting across from him.

The man to the warden's left had fluffy eyebrows that made up for the lack of hair on his head. His face was oval like an egg. His short neck was punctuated by a purple bowtie that matched the handkerchief in his seersucker jacket. Unlike the superintendent, he stared directly at Victor.

"He looks like a mad scientist," James said. "He must be an administrator."

In contrast, the warden's chiseled face glimmered in the light pouring into the room through the floor-to-ceiling windows. A tailored pinstriped suit and gray tie hung from his lean frame. He adjusted the circular glasses resting atop his protruding nose and stared at Prisoner #1030 in disgust. Victor was sporting a baggy inmate's uniform. While the warden couldn't chastise him for wearing prison-issued attire, Hitchcock was repulsed to have such degrading clothes worn in the only room at Watermill that epitomized sophisticated grandeur. The Crane had personally attended to every detail of the conference room adjacent to his office, including the Versailles-inspired crystal chandelier and the hand-carved mantel bookended by cherubs.

"I'm not so sure that angels are the appropriate decoration for the warden," James said and quoted from Shakespeare's *The Tempest,* another of Lily's favorite plays: "Hell is empty and all the devils are here."

Without any formal introductions, the two men sitting on either side of the warden took turns pelting rapid-fire questions at Victor.

"Where are you from?" the bald man asked.

"New York."

"Where in New York?" mustached man asked.

"Emerson."

"What is your former profession?"

"Teacher."

"What kind of teacher?"

"I taught English."

"Are you married?"

"Not anymore."

"Do you socialize and interact with other inmates?"

"Occasionally."

"What happened on Old River Way?"

"There was a car crash. I was the driver."

"Were you intoxicated?"

"Yes — I was."

"Why did you drink so much alcohol if you knew you were going to drive?"

"I ask myself that question every day."

"Do you remember killing James St. George?"

"No."

"Are you sorry for what you've done?"

"More than you'll ever know."

"Do you think you'd do it again?"

"No."

The warden sat in satisfied silence and watched his lackeys verbally torture Victor. He wondered if Prisoner #1030, whose face was turning red, would snap under the pressure. Victor's heartbeat quickened, and he felt a burning in his chest. He swallowed hard and was about to fire back at the interrogators when he was startled by a hand on his shoulder. He jerked back his head in surprise, but no one was there. His anger morphed to anxiety.

Could I have imagined it?

He heard a voice.

"Keep a cool head. It's all a game."

"Is something wrong?" the interviewers asked in unison. The warden raised his eyebrows.

"No," Victor responded with confidence. "I'm fine."

"Good," the bald man said. "Let's continue with the questions."

"What do you dislike most about your incarceration?" the mustached man asked.

"The inability to make my own choices."

"Do you enjoy working in the prison library?" the

bald man asked.

"I do."

"Why do you like the library?"

"Solitude. Books. Words."

"Have you ever violated the warden's code of conduct?"

Victor ignored the question and let his mind drift to the smell wafting into the room from the forest. It tickled his nostrils. Alyssum? Probably not. Gardenias? Maybe. The guards told him they were abundant in the valley below. The voice in his head returned.

"It's flowering dogwood from the garden."

That must be it — flowering dogwood. Victor appreciated the garden, especially the flowers he planted. He considered gardening one of his few positive contributions to the prison.

"Are you listening, Mr. Young?" the warden asked in a stern voice. He fidgeted with the glasses resting on his nose. "Mr. Perkins and Mr. Peters asked you a question. Are you going to answer them? You may have all of the time in the world, but we do not. I would like this parole hearing to conclude sooner rather than later. We all have important things to do."

Victor ignored the warden's diatribe and returned to ruminating about the flowery scent.

"There are so many varieties of dogwood," he said. "You can find them on the edge of the forest. They're plentiful in this part of the country. I've become a horticulture connoisseur of sorts following my work in the garden. The irony is that I had to be sent to prison to learn about something so wild, beautiful and free. Did you know the dense trunk of the dogwood tree is used to make cutting boards?"

The three men sitting across the table stared back in dumbfounded silence.

"Dogwood is most spectacular during the fall foliage. I can see the trees through the window in my cell."

The warden interrupted Victor.

"You've served 16 years of a 20-year sentence, and you've done, shall we say…" The warden paused to find the right word. "Satisfactory work in the library and records room. To this day, I still don't know how you were able to find the Harvey Lotion file."

"Did the warden compliment you?" James asked.

"However, there were numerous instances where my staff couldn't locate you when you were supposed to be on your shift. Where were you hiding?"

Victor shrugged.

"I can't say, warden. I split my time between my cell and the library. There's nowhere else for me to go."

Hitchcock shot the inmate a dubious glance.

"In any event, aside from some instances of violence where the blame doesn't fall directly at your feet, you have a record of good behavior. That's more than I can say about the other inhabitants in this correctional facility. Still, I find your introverted ways unhealthy and eccentric."

The warden slid his glasses down his hooked nose, exhaled onto the lenses and wiped them on his skinny tie.

"Mr. Young, if I can properly recall, you're the only inmate I've encountered at this institution who's never inquired about early release. I was told that you only became aware of this hearing when my office sent you a written notice. Why have you never asked about it? Don't you want to go home?"

No one had ever asked him that question. Victor's previous life had floated away long ago like pollen in a windstorm. No sense trying to find the scattered petals. Home was gone, and he wouldn't even know where to begin looking for it.

"You should say something," James urged. "This could be your chance."

The spirit guide was taken aback by his own advice. He wanted the best for his friend — that's how he thought of Victor all these years later. Forgiveness had released him from pain. The anger he experienced after he died was gone. More importantly, the pact he'd forged with God remained intact: the weathered inmate before him was alive and well.

"It's time to leave this place," James whispered into Victor's ear. "It's time for the next adventure."

The pot-bellied man with the bushy mustache interrupted the silence with a bellicose rumble.

"There's still chance for redemption," he said. "It's never too late."

Victor scratched his forehead.

"The truth is I'll never be able redeem myself for killing that young man. I don't know much about James St. George, only what I've read in the newspapers. I keep his photograph in my pocket because it reminds me of the life I took. No amount of penance will rid my soul of regret. I've tried to forgive myself, but I can't. The burden is too great, and if serving my full prison sentence fulfills my debt to God, then so be it."

Victor walked toward the window and opened it

wider. The three men in suits scrunched their faces in annoyance at the inmate's audacity.

"I pray every day," Victor continued.

Hitchcock shifted uncomfortably in his chair.

"It's funny because I never prayed until I got here — no such thing as an atheist in a foxhole, right? Finding God in a place like this is what's gotten me through the long days and nights."

The warden was not amused. He believed inmates lost their societal rights when they committed heinous crimes, and that included the right to practice religion. His no-religion decree may have violated their constitutional rights, but the only constitution that mattered inside the Watermill Correctional Facility was the one penned by Rufus Covington Hitchcock III. Unbeknownst to the warden, the guards had discarded boxes of confiscated Bibles in the library, and during a cursory search for records, a certain librarian stumbled upon the sacred books and put many of them back into circulation.

James knew Victor had become spiritual but was unaware his relationship with God was robust enough to defend in front of a godless dictator who had no use for inmates with "philosophies" as he called them.

"Philosophies spread like wildfire," Hitchcock once told the guards. "If you don't keep them under control, they'll burn down the whole damn building. It's more dangerous than any gang because if others take to the ridiculousness, then who knows what kind of mayhem will ensue?"

"I lived another life before this one," Victor told the suits. "I taught literature to high school students. F. Scott Fitzgerald was my favorite, and I loved seeing my student's excitement when they read *The Great Gatsby* or *This Side of Paradise*.

His voice dropped.

"I was married too. She was the most beautiful women I'd ever met. The last time I saw her was at my trial. She left me for another man, but I don't blame her for leaving. I pushed her away when I drove drunk and killed James. I didn't deserve her."

Victor fell back into his chair at the end of the table.

"Our lives are like balls of yarn, good and bad intertwined together. My life's been filled with more bad than good, but I believe I can salvage what's left."

Unsettling silence filled the space. The warden stared hard at Prisoner #1030. He pushed back his wooden chair. His wingtips clicked against the floor as he strolled across the room. He moved more like a limping bird than a man. The administrators eyed his gangly walk. Hitchcock pressed his fists to the mahogany table, leaned in and whispered into the inmate's ear, "Get the hell out of my prison."

CHAPTER 14
HOME SWEET HOME

The shared apartment in the halfway house had more cobwebs than furniture. In Victor's shoebox of a bedroom, a ceramic lamp missing a lampshade sat on a walnut nightstand that hadn't been moved in years as evident by the deep indentation in the brown carpet. A twin bed pushed into the corner had musty sheets, a jungle-green blanket and a flattened pillow — not much different from his prison cell. A dinged-up wooden folding chair was propped against the wall. The mesh weave that made up the seat was brittle and had holes. Victor feared if he sat down, he'd fall right through. The only saving grace was the room's built-in shelves, which were lined with books: *The Adventures of Huckleberry Finn*, *The Catcher in the Rye* and *Moby Dick*. At least there's something to read, he thought. Victor ran his index finger across the book covers and accumulated a thick coating of dust that danced in the beams of sunlight shining in through the window. He sneezed.

"I can't say I've seen one of these in a long time," James said, pointing to a boxy television with rabbit-ear antennas resting atop a small table. While Victor never watched TV in prison — he wanted to avoid the other inmates — he did notice that the TVs hanging on the wall in the rec room were flat. This was one was bulky.

"Do you think it works?" James asked. They both stared at the object like they'd unearthed buried treasure. Victor touched the glass screen — more dust.

"Let's turn it on and see what happens," the spirit guide said.

Victor found a remote control on the nightstand and pointed it at the TV but no luck.

"Batteries must be dead," he said and opened the back panel to jostle the crusted cylinders, which looked like they hadn't been changed in decades. Maybe this will do the trick? When he tried the remote a second time, the ancient box came alive. Muted colors pierced the grimy film.

"I can't believe it still works," Victor said as he flipped through the channels.

Everything on the screen looked foreign. There was a dating game show, an infomercial hawking a portable printer that wirelessly connected to a computer and a broadcast of a Yankees-Red Sox game. Victor was an avid sports fan and loved baseball as much as soccer but recognized none of the players on the field. For the past 16 years, he'd been locked in a concrete time capsule with little knowledge of what was happening in the outside world, including the famous baseball rivalry between New York and Boston.

"What a play!" an announcer shouted. "Nelson jumps over the wall to rob the batter of a home run. I bet the Yankees' pitcher will buy that outfielder a pitcher of beer after the game. As we head into the last inning of play, we're all tied up — Yankees 3 Red Sox 3!"

Lily had been a Yankees fan, so by default James pulled for the pinstripes, but like his friend, he knew none of the players. Victor turned off the TV and stared anxiously at the blank screen unsure what to do next.

"Fill her up with regular," a deep voice bellowed.

Victor and James peered out of the bedroom window and watched a young gas-station attendant covered in tattoos service a red convertible. The driver retracted the roof as the teen pumped gasoline into the sports car.

"What a beauty," Victor said with a grin, the first time he'd smiled since being released.

"Maybe we'll get to drive something like that one day," James said. He loved cars as much as Victor and missed his pickup truck, a beat-up machine with more dings to count. At the time of his death, it was pushing 200,000 miles and was still going strong. He wondered what had happen to it.

Victor's assigned housing was situated above a noisy auto-body shop with gas pumps out front. Wrenches, sanders and grinders buzzed as the mechanics replaced engine blocks, repaired fuel injectors and fixed every other problem under the hood. Invariably at 5 o'clock, the work stopped — a welcome respite from the mechanical music — and everyone went home. For some, that meant walking upstairs to the halfway house.

The shop was situated along Old River Way, several miles east of Emerson. The two-story brick building was the only spot where locals would agree to house newly-released prisoners, far away from the center of town. Emerson's residents were leery of ex-cons living and working near their homes. The old man who owned the auto body shop got money from the state for providing lodging to the former felons, and in return, he paid them to pump gas and do odd jobs. Some learned how to fix cars as opposed to stealing them. It was all part of their integration back into society. The warden required quarterly reports on the inmates' progress until probation expired. That meant four more years of checking in for Victor, who'd returned to the place where his life had changed forever. The old stone bridge was only a few miles down the road.

James watched the sports car rocket out of the gas station and down the winding road, leaving a plume of dust in its path. It roared into the hills and disappeared behind the pine trees. The rumbling engine faded as it drove deeper into the countryside. Victor also watched, but with apprehension. A knot in the pit of his stomach tightened, and his palms were sweaty. He felt the eyes of the teenage gas station attendant from below. He closed the dusty curtains and moved to his bed.

Victor slept little his first night as a free man and tossed and turned for hours. He half-expected a guard to sound-off for evening count, but there were no guards, no yelling, no bars and no unusual noises coming from the shadows. He opened the creaky door to his bedroom and peered down the dark hallway. His bare feet stuck to the wood floor as he stepped into the kitchen. He filled a glass with water from the tap, but when he brought the cup to his lips, his shaky hand spilled the drink on the counter.

An owl outside the kitchen window hooted underneath the cloudless sky. Victor looked through the dirty pane of glass and glanced up at the stars, millions of bright, beautiful, shining stars. So many stars. He tried to find the Little Dipper and Polaris, but his concentration was poor, and he couldn't focus.

There was little James could do to assuage Victor's nerves. The spirit guide was also uneasy being back in Emerson. He wondered what he might find in his old town. He wondered if he'd see Lily walking the promenade, or serving drinks at The Dragon's Den, or lounging on the college green with a stack of books.

But he knew she was long gone and so was everyone else.

*

Victor's worldly possessions were minimal. He'd stuffed everything he owned into a canvas bag that one of the guards gave him when he left Watermill. There wasn't much inside of it — more keepsakes than valuables. The pinstripe suit he wore for his trial was buried at the bottom. At the time, it was brand new but now was wrinkled and stale. There was no reason to keep it.

"It's more banker than high school teacher," James said.

Victor searched the lapel pocket of the suit jacket for the jewelry he'd hidden. His eyes flashed with excitement — it was still there. Did the guards not search his clothing before they stuffed it away in a container? He was certain they would've stolen the gold crucifix as well as his grandfather's watch. Victor examined the necklace. Prior to being sent to prison, he wore it every day but chose not to keep it at Watermill. No need to attract unwanted attention. Inmates would steal anything valuable. Plus, he wanted to avoid angering the warden.

The cross felt cold, yet familiar on his bare chest. He'd forgotten how much he missed it. Victor snapped the watch on his left wrist. The minute and hour hands were stuck at 1:11 a.m. The glass bezel was scratched. He tapped the black face to jump-start the internal mechanisms but had no success. Even though the timepiece was a reminder of his sins, he liked wearing it. It made him feel normal again.

"Maybe a new battery will do the trick," James said. "The pharmacy at the corner of the town square should have one."

A new battery could be the fix. He'd missed his watch. At Watermill, time was a luxury the inmates were denied. The warden banned wrist watches and removed all of the hanging clocks throughout the facility. The guards were the only ones with watches, and therefore dictated when it was time to eat, work and sleep. Time became a weapon. Victor appreciated the irony — the men with all the time in the world were deprived the right to keep it.

Also inside the duffel bag, Victor found his leather wallet, and behind a washed out $10 bill, a folded photo of he and his ex-wife smiling in front of a barn. They were wearing boots, jeans and matching sweaters. The photo had been their Christmas card that season — their last Christmas together.

"She's beautiful," James said.

It was the first time he'd seen a picture of Kristen, and in many ways, she reminded him of Lily. Both women exuded warm glows with full smiles. A tear rolled down Victor's cheek and plopped onto the photo. He wiped it off with his finger but smudged the ink and rushed to pat the picture on his pants. Kristen's smile was salvaged. He opened the drawer to his nightstand and slid the picture inside. After the Dear John letter, Victor never heard from Kristen again and knew he never would.

"I know how hard it is to lose someone you love," the spirit guide said. "I think about Lily all of the time."

Victor shook his head in disgust and tossed the duffel bag in the corner of his tiny room. The landlord had built partitions to convert what was a two-bedroom apartment into four rooms. It was a clear violation of building code, but a few bribes to unscrupulous town supervisors apathetic to the living conditions of ex-cons, and the building magically passed inspection.

"It's better than a prison cell, so they should be thrilled," a town councilman said.

All of the occupants in the apartment shared a galley kitchen and one cramped bathroom. The edge of the toilet was in the pathway of the door, so it never closed properly and required a gymnastics-like maneuver to navigate to the cramped shower. The drafty apartment was cramped, but Victor couldn't afford an alternative. There was little left in his bank account following the divorce, and most of his life savings had gone to pay for his defense attorney.

His roommates included a 62-year-old car thief nicknamed Gumby, who worked as a mechanic in the garage downstairs. Gumby had served several stretches at Watermill for grand theft auto, so he enjoyed being around cars. As one of the mechanics would later explain to Victor, Gumby earned his nickname for his ability to hide in confined spaces. If an auto heist went bust and cops showed up, Gumby would slide underneath cars, behind garbage cans or even inside oil barrels to elude capture. He'd stay hidden for as long as necessary, even hours, and would use darkness as cover to slip away into the night, never to be seen until the next job. His diminutive stature made his acrobatic feats possible. Standing 5 feet 2 inches and 120 pounds, Gumby was more race-horse jockey than hardened criminal. But age, poor health and a botched car theft forced the auto thief into an early retirement.

In contrast, Vladimir was a foot and a half taller than Gumby. The day laborer from Russia had served time for beating a man nearly to death. The fight happened outside a club where Vladimir worked as a bouncer. The Russian tossed the drunk out of the bar and proceeded to pummel him with his fists in the middle of the street. When the police asked him why he beat the man so brutally, Vladimir explained, "He insulted my mother." Like Gumby, he too had a job. The Russian was a tractor operator at a nearby farm.

The third roommate was a runaway teen with piercings that outnumbered tattoos. His head was perpetually on a tilt to keep his stringy, jet-black hair from covering his obsidian eyes. He did more staring than talking.

"Hi, my name is Victor," he said to his younger roommate one afternoon in the cramped kitchen. "I recently moved in from Watermill. What's your name?"

The expressionless teen cloaked in black removed his TV dinner from the microwave and dropped the hotplate on the counter. He took off the plastic wrapping that covered the meatloaf, mashed potatoes and brownie. After a minute of uncomfortable silence, he shot an annoyed glance at the former teacher, who still prided himself on interacting with young people.

"Where are you from?" Victor asked in a high-pitch voice as if he was talking to a puppy.

The teen turned his back, left the kitchen with his rubbery food and disappeared into a bedroom.

"At least, he's friendly," James said.

*

For more than a week, Victor avoided venturing outside the halfway house and preferred lounging around the cramped, dark apartment, even though there was little room to lounge. In-between reading *Invisible Man* and *Othello*, he tried to pass the time by chatting with his ex-con roommates, but his attempts at conversation proved fruitless.

Vladimir spoke little English, and it remained unclear if the name-less, tattooed teen communicated verbally at all. Victor had yet to meet Gumby but had the pleasure of cleaning up after him. The aging ex-car thief left trails of used cigarettes from the living room to his bedroom. Some butts were stuffed out in tea cups and others were left to burn away on the window sill. Victor looked forward to chastising his new roommate for his dirty habits.

In the meantime, he endured the stifling humidity and wiped away sweat from his forehead. A heat wave had gripped the area and made physical activity of any sort unbearable. Victor had escaped hell only to feel as though he'd been dropped back into the middle of it. The 90-degree heat sapped his energy. He pressed a glass filled with diet soda and ice cubes to his cheek. His hot skin melted the ice. There was one air conditioner in the entire apartment, and it stuck out of the kitchen window. The ancient machine chugged loudly and was only effective in cooling a three-foot radius. Beyond that, the cold air failed to circulate.

"It's maxed out," a shirtless Victor said.

Living above an auto-body shop filled with equipment and hot metal didn't help the situation. Victor gulped down his soda and chewed on the ice in his glass.

"I feel like we're baking in an oven," James said. Maybe it was the heat or an urge to tackle the unavoidable, but the spirit guide made a suggestion he'd been dreading.

"It's time we walk into town."

That would entail crossing the old stone bridge. There was no way to avoid it. James felt anxious even thinking about it. So did Victor, who chewed on more ice. The former teacher avoided drinking alcohol following the crash but felt an immediate urge to down whiskey to calm the nerves. Booze was banned in prison and acquiring it through back channels was a tricky endeavor. When he did have opportunities to drink smuggled beer at Watermill, he declined because he was too ashamed.

"We've got to do it sooner or later, so we might as well do it now," James said.

The ex-con's sweaty skin peeled off the back of the wooden chair in the kitchen as he stood up. His back and knees cracked. The hair on his chest was gray. His legs ached. He squeezed into a white T-shirt and grabbed his wallet and door keys.

James smiled at his older friend. Victor's age was a testament to the spirit guide's success. Victor was alive and well. He'd survived Watermill and escaped mostly unscathed, but even James recognized that their journey together was far from complete.

CHAPTER 15
WALKING INTO THE PAST

The brass knob on the apartment's front door taunted Victor. He glared at it, shifted his weight and tapped his fingers against his thigh. The pace of the tapping quickened. He took a deep breath, stretched out his arm and lingered for several seconds before grabbing the door handle.

It was time to go.

Victor walked down a flight of steps that led him to the parking lot of Emerson Auto Body. The gravel in the driveway crackled underneath his feet like kernels of popcorn on a hot stove. The humid air had a faint whiff of gasoline from pools of spilled fuel near the pumps. A sign read $2.50 per unleaded gallon. Inflation had skyrocketed since he'd been locked up.

The shop was open for business, but with no cars to service, the motley crew of crooks turned auto mechanics lounged on upside-down buckets, puffed on cigarettes and sucked down beer. They eyed the skinny ex-con with a slight hunch as he sauntered past them. Victor gave a half-hearted wave. No one reciprocated.

"Don't worry about them," James said. "They're bad news."

Victor stepped from the driveway onto the paved road. His legs felt wobbly. He peered up at a green street sign covered by overgrowth and took a deep breath, inhaling the soupy air. Underneath the vines, the white lettering was still visible: Old River Way.

"We're in this together," James said. He put his arm around Victor and propped him up as they embarked on their trek down the rural road leading to the center of town. Clouds that looked like giant cotton balls stood out against a light-blue canvas. Wheat fields flanked them on either side. The 5-foot tall stalks swayed in the summer wind and reminded James of the farm he saw in heaven, the one across the river from where Grandpa was fishing. Maybe he was closer to returning home than he thought.

In nature's solitude, the former school teacher and his spirit guide heeded the whispers of the countryside. A bluebird darted past them at lighting speed. Its feathered body was the same color as the sea. Its chest was as brown as a tree trunk. The bird rested atop a wheat stalk before shooting onward toward town.

"I think we've got a shadow," James said. "He's been following us since the gas station. It's a good omen."

When he and his brother were growing up, their mother told them that colorful animals were signs from the angels. James sure hoped that was the case because he could certainly use their help.

The scent of manure grew stronger. A herd of cows chomped on grass and lifted their bulky heads to watch the strangers meander down the country road, but the massive creatures quickly lost interest and returned to snacking on the earth. The sight of dairy cows brought a smile to Victor's face. He'd long forgotten what they looked like because he hadn't seen a cow in years. Meanwhile, James was more fascinated by the sprinkler contraptions on wheels that farmers used to water their crops.

"They look like giant airplane wings, and they're as long as football fields. Lily and I walked this road all of the time, and I don't ever remember seeing them."

The bluebird whizzed past Victor's head a second time and nearly clipped his ear.

"What the…"

He ducked and prepared for another aerial assault, but it never came.

"He wants us to follow him," James said. "He's leading the way."

The road curved into the forest and snaked underneath a canopy of tree branches that filtered the sunlight and provided much-needed shade. Victor and James soaked in the plethora of color engulfing them from all sides — a saturated beauty that delighted the senses. The simplest things were the most spectacular: a frog leaping over a log; green moss clinging to a tree; cicadas chirping together to create a melody; a stag meandering through the woods. James counted the antler tines; it was a 12-point buck. He thought back to his bow and arrow hunt with Grandpa. There was no way he could kill something so majestic. The deer disappeared behind a cluster of birch trees, and they continued their march forward, following the road down a hill toward their destiny.

When the old stone bridge came into view, it dared them to venture across. Victor's heart beat quickened. A trickle of tears dripped down his cheeks and fell to the hot pavement. He dropped to his knees and pressed his hands to the ground. His body shook as if he had a fever.

"I can't do it," he whispered.

He remembered little of what happened that night. The alcohol coursing through his blood had muddled his memory. He could only recall stumbling out of his car and cursing at the mangled mess. After vomiting into the river, he whipped around to face a police officer. That's where it all gets hazy. His lawyer told him that he took a swing at the cop and landed a punch square on the officer's jaw. Victor's swollen wrist throbbed the next morning when he awoke in a holding cell.

"I always thought it was the most beautiful spot in town and never would've imagined it'd be the place where I'd die," James said. "I heard your engine rumbling in the darkness, but when I turned around it was too late. No time to get out of the way. I know you didn't hit me on purpose. Wrong place at the wrong time. Funny how that happens."

"I never meant to hit anyone," Victor said. Tears streamed from his puffy eyes. "It was an accident…. a terrible accident."

James squeezed Victor's boney shoulder. There was little muscle to grab.

"I forgive you. The past is the past. It's about time we get to the other side of the bridge — wouldn't you say?"

Victor took a deep breath, stood up, crossed himself and stepped onto the uneven stones. Each had a unique contour, color and shape. He remembered how his car slid across the bumpy surface. The tires failed to gain traction and instead of slowing down, he hit the gas to go faster, too drunk to know what he was doing. That's when he lost control.

The river flowed underneath the bridge and rippled over enormous rocks poking through the water's surface. A school of trout navigated downstream and left a trail of bubbles in their wake. Nature's peaceful symphony was a sharp contrast to the havoc all those years ago.

When they reached the peak of the arch bridge, James rubbed his hand along the stone edge where the car hit his body. The impact of the crash had damaged the masonry and left deep gouges — physical reminders of a horror etched in time. He studied the exact spot where his lifeless body was sprawled out on the stone: clothes tattered; bones broken; heart lacerated.

The spirit guide had expected to feel sorry for himself; his goals and dreams curtailed by recklessness. Instead, he was motivated to cross the bridge with Victor by his side. He'd been lucky enough to see heaven and knew what and who was waiting for him on the other side. If helping Victor was his ticket home, then so be it.

James spotted an elderly woman painting the landscape along the banks of the river. Her canvas was propped up on an easel, which had a ledge to hold watercolors. He remembered walking past her on his way to work. Like James, she hadn't aged a day. She smiled back, and James reciprocated. There were spirit guides and angels everywhere.

James peered down at his old stomping grounds. The Dragon's Den had been replaced by a café with outdoor seating. A man sipping an expresso pounded away on a silver laptop, while a young woman lounging in a chair read the newspaper.

"The Dragon's Den was where I met Lily and so many of my friends. Little Gerry was a big hit. Everyone wanted to play with him, and I think he enjoyed the attention."

James's thoughts were interrupted by a buzzing near his right ear. The bluebird had returned.

"It's good to see you again," he said.

The colorful bird escorted them across the second half of the bridge. When they stepped off the stone and onto the blacktop, their hearts flickered with relief. They'd faced their greatest fear and conquered it. Time to keep walking.

All the shops clustered around the town square had colorful façades. A pink building sat adjacent to a brick building painted lime green, which was connected to a yellow, colonial-style building with porches at each of its three levels. There was a tailor, baker, barber and butcher. The businesses surrounded a Greek Revival courthouse with Doric columns, a tiered dome and a broken four-sided clock in the tower: the hour and minute hand remained perpetually stuck in vertical positions, both pointing at twelve. James always cursed the broken clock whenever he was late to class. The town council had hired a master clockmaker to examine its mechanics, but the repair estimate came in well over budget. A specialized crane was needed to hoist heavy replacement gears high into the sky. So, the clock assumed an ornamental role rather than a functional one. The multi-purpose building housed the police department, tax assessor, records, library, animal control and every other office a small town would need. Victor shuddered as he walked in its shadow — too many unpleasant memories from the trial.

He and James visited more than a dozen shops in the square with the intention of finding a watch battery and a job. There was always the fallback of repairing cars or pumping gas at the auto body shop, but neither appealed much to the former teacher. Not because he thought the work was beneath him — he valued cars as much as books — rather he needed to distance himself from the others who reminded him of a past he was trying to escape. But Victor's quest for employment was proving unproductive. While most of the business owners he met were cordial, none offered any work, and he soon realized few people in town trusted ex-cons.

"I don't need any help," the tailor said. "I can manage on my own."

The baker delivered a similar line.

"Fully staffed," the man said. His white apron had an embroidered image of a cake. "But take one of our donuts before you leave. They're the most famous in the county! It's on the house."

Victor took the baker up on his offer and snatched a jelly donut. The sweet raspberry oozed out of its core. True to the baker's word, it was a piece of sugary heaven.

The owner of the tavern was less affable.

"Don't need no help," the grumpy man spat through his missing teeth. The faded tattoos on his arms were lumps of indistinguishable green ink. A boat anchor? A mermaid? Something maritime, perhaps? James pulled up his own sleeve to compare tattoos.

"I'm sure you could use the extra help," Victor pleaded. "I can cook, clean and even make drinks." He stopped himself. The idea of serving alcohol made him uneasy. "Well maybe not bartender, but I can do other things."

"We're doing good on our own," the surly man barked. He waddled toward the kitchen. "No need to bring on more people when the ship is floating just fine. We're the only joint in town since The Dragon's Den closed."

"When did it shut down?" Victor asked.

"Maybe a decade ago. Look, you're wasting my time, and like I said, I don't need no help. I got things to do in the kitchen, so you can show yourself out."

He stumbled through a set of swinging doors and left Victor and James alone inside the dingy tavern.

"He was pleasant, wouldn't you say?" James said.

"I don't know what to do next."

The rejections continued throughout the day, and Victor accepted that he'd likely be forced to ask for shifts repairing cars.

"Why don't we make one more stop before giving up?" James suggested. "Let's swing by the pharmacy. We can ask about work and check on that watch battery."

The reflection of the pulsating sunset, a conflagration of reds and oranges in the front window, is what caught Victor's attention. A maroon sign that read "Sterling Pharmacy" hung by rusty chains from the porch's ceiling. It creaked as it swung in the wind. The pharmacy seemed like a good place to end the day, and Victor decided to give it one last shot. A bell dinged when he opened the shop's door. The musty smell reminded him of his grandmother's house, where all of the living room furniture was covered in plastic.

"May I help you?" a frail woman asked from behind the register. Her high-pitched voice cracked as she pronounced every constant and syllable. "We're closing soon but will stay open until you find what you need."

A fake set of white teeth made up all of her sweet smile. Her light-green eyes looked like two shiny gems trapped in an aging body. The woman's eclectic shop was filled with everything from medicine to greeting cards to plastic vampire teeth to screwdrivers and hammers. Luckily for Victor, there were also batteries for watches. He picked out the one he needed.

"Ma'am, I appreciate your hospitality," he said and handed the elderly shopkeeper a $5 bill. He tapped his fingers on the checkout counter.

"I must admit I didn't just come here to shop. I was also curious about..." He stammered, almost too embarrassed to ask. "Well... I was curious... do you need any help here?"

The pharmacist mixing medications in the back of the store peered over at the stranger.

"I'm a good worker and can do a lot of things." He hesitated, unsure how much to tell her. "The truth is I got to town a week ago. I live above the auto body shop on Old River Way."

Victor figured he didn't need to say much more.

Everyone in town knew about the halfway house. As he prepared himself for yet another rejection, the old woman shuffled her feet and walked around the counter while humming a tune. It carried out of the open window. Everyone who walked by the pharmacy could hear her singing.

"This is interesting," she said.

Her bushy-gray hair bounced when she moved. She got within inches of Victor's face and poked him in the chest with two fingers.

"I had a feeling someone like you would walk into my shop today. It sounds like we're about to talk business, and I never talk business before my afternoon tea. Would you care to join me on the front porch?"

"Yes, ma'am," Victor said with surprise.

It wasn't the response he was expecting. He put out his arm and escorted the frail shopkeeper onto the porch and into a cushioned-wicker chair. Not since Jose could he remember anyone who'd showed him kindness.

"It's not easy getting old," she said. "My body doesn't move the way it once did, but I've accepted that. I've had a good run and can't complain." Her cackle startled the birds resting on a tree, and they took off in flight.

"She reminds me of Grandpa," James said.

After they settled into their seats, the front door swung open, and the gangly pharmacist carried out a silver tray with two tea cups, a kettle filled with hot water, a bowl of brown sugar cubes, sliced lemons and spoons.

"Thank you, Ed," she said.

The pharmacist nodded, and without saying a

word, slipped back into the shop. The elderly woman dumped a spoonful of sugar into her tea cup.

"A generous helping?" Victor said with a smile.

"Nothing can ever be too sweet. The same is true in life. You need the sweet to balance out the sour, and sweetie…" Her voice quieted. "There's way too much sour."

"You don't need to tell me." Victor poured himself some tea and wrapped his fingers around the tiny cup. "It's just that I never thought life could be filled with this much sour."

"Those bumps in the road brought you to this point in time, so whether you know it or not, you're fulfilling your destiny."

The old woman stretched out her wrinkled hand.

"My name is Donna Pearl Sterling, but everyone in town calls me Ms. Sterling."

"It's a pleasure to meet you Ms. Sterling. My name is Victor Young."

"Victor as in Victor Frankenstein?"

"Yes, but not exactly. My father named me after the French writer, not the mad doctor who created the monster."

"*The Hunchback of Notre Dame* is one of my favorites. Are you like the hunchback, Mr. Young?"

Victor was taken aback by the question. He'd never been compared to the half-blind bell-ringer Quasimodo.

"Ma'am, in many ways, I guess you could say I am."

"We all have our burdens, Mr. Young. For me, it was Jack's death."

She explained how her husband started the business a half-century ago, and the shop had remained a staple in town ever since, fitting perfectly into the landscape of the square. The chain pharmacies had yet to encroach on Emerson, in part because the council blocked them from planting roots, a decision that protected her jewel.

"This shop is Jack's legacy," she explained. "I guess that's why I keep it going. Closing it down would mean letting a piece of him die. After the cancer took him from me, I vowed to run the pharmacy."

"My condolences."

"Thank you," she said and gazed into her tea cup as if she was waiting for a sign.

"I feel his spirit guiding me. We all have a spirit guide, you know. Do you like your tea?"

"Very much, ma'am," Victor said. "I haven't had anything so sweet since prison."

Ms. Sterling smiled with satisfaction.

"Mr. Young, why do you want to work here?"

Victor sighed.

"The truth is I haven't had much luck convincing anyone to hire me. The idea of having an ex-convict around cash and valuables isn't appealing for many business owners, and I don't fault them. But I want a job to…"

He stuttered.

"…feel normal again."

"He needs a second chance," James blurted. "Deep down, he's a good person."

"Everyone deserves second chances, even those of us who've committed the worst of sins," she said.

Ms. Sterling peered through the pharmacy's window and stared at the awkward man counting pills at the counter, the same one who'd brought them tea on a tray.

"Is Ed a former inmate too?" James asked.

The lanky figure in the lab coat mixed a pink liquid underneath a harsh, white light. Every few seconds, the fluorescent tubes above him on the ceiling flickered.

"That's my pharmacist, Ed. He's been with me for a long time."

She shouted through the open window.

"Ed, how many years have you worked here?"

The pharmacist shrugged.

"Would you like to come over and introduce yourself?"

Ed removed his glasses and squinted indifferently at Victor before returning to his pill counting. He slid a dozen capsules into a translucent plastic bottle with an orange tinge.

"He's a loquacious man," James said. "Does he know what he's doing?"

"Ed's as smart as they come, probably smarter than all of us combined! I don't know how he was able to focus in prison and study pharmacology. When he was released, he completed all of his coursework and certifications. It's amazing how he rebounded following the murder."

"Murder?" Victor and James said in unison.

Ms. Sterling lowered her voice.

"He's not a monster. I can promise you that."

"What did he do?" James asked.

"If there's one thing I've learned in my 91 years of life, it's that there's a constant battle between good and evil. Good always prevails, but every now and then, evil wins a battle. Ed experienced evil at a young age. He was the oldest child in a family ruled by an abusive drunk. Poor Ed would show up to school with bruises and black eyes. When his teachers asked him what happened, he lied and made up a story. He never wanted his father to get into trouble. As much as he hated his dad, he still loved him. His mother and younger sister took the brunt of the beatings.

"When Ed was 14 years old, he came home from baseball practice and found his mama on the kitchen floor, and his sister lying across the coffee table in the living room. Both had been bludgeoned to death. In a fit of drunken rage, his papa had smashed an iron skillet across their heads. He was upset the trash hadn't been taken out."

James's eyes widened with horror.

"Ed grabbed a 12-gauge shotgun from the coat closet and carried it into the wood shed, where he found his father sobbing at the work bench and nursing a bottle of whiskey. He confessed and told Ed he was sorry for what he'd done, but anger overcame Ed's broken spirit. He pointed the shotgun at his father and..."

Ms. Sterling's voice trailed off.

James and Victor sat in stunned silence.

"His lawyer argued self-defense and claimed years of emotional and physical abuse had driven him to kill. Maybe Ed saved his own life before his father had a chance of taking it, but in the end, he committed murder. A 14-year-old boy with a loaded shotgun delivered his own brand of justice. Prosecutors charged him as an adult, but the judge was lenient. Four years in juvenile detention, and when he turned 18, two years at Watermill. When he was released, they sent him to the same halfway house where you're living. My husband hired him to clean the floors, and after he passed his pharmacy certification test, he promoted Ed. A flawless pharmacist. Never makes a mistake."

Ed arched the left side of his lip in a smirk.

"He hasn't spoken since he killed his father," she continued. "He wouldn't even talk to his lawyers, which made defending him a challenge. But he communicates in his own way. It's hard to recover from something like that."

Victor couldn't explain it, but he felt at ease with Ms. Sterling. Maybe it was her grandmotherly ways. Maybe it was having someone to talk to again after such a long stretch of solitude. He'd lost his best friend when Jose died.

"I wasted away in prison," he admitted. "I'm not complaining about my punishment. I got what I deserved, and I'm not sure whether I deserve redemption."

"We all deserve redemption," she said. "But more about that later — I thought we were here to discuss a job."

CHAPTER 16
A LIFE OF ROUTINES

The alarm shrieked at 6:00 a.m. Victor swung his arm to hit the off button and nearly knocked over the lamp on his nightstand. The noisy clock was as obnoxious as the wake-up special at Watermill, when a guard would drag his nightstick across the iron bars and hit each in succession like a mallet to a xylophone — BANG, BANG, BANG, BANG.

"Morning, ladies!" he'd shout with a caustic grin. The other corrections officers laughed as inmates jolted awake out of a deep sleep. Some even fell from their bunks and landed on the concrete floor. The tortured prisoners plotted their revenge in secret.

When he was an inmate, Victor longed for an alarm clock, but now that he had one, he cursed it every morning. Its cacophony pierced his eardrums, and he fantasized about smashing it into a thousand pieces. Against his better judgement, he went to Vladimir for help.

"Why need hammer?" asked his Russian

roommate, who had as much hair on his hands and chest as his beard. James thought he looked more bear than human.

"I'm hanging a coat hook in my room," Victor lied. "Do you have one?"

His hairy roommate raised his eyebrows and tapped his chin in pensive thought.

"Don't have one but can get one. No problem. But don't use for stealing car. Better tools for that."

James rolled his eyes.

"Once a thief, always a thief," he said. "If you ask this guy for a favor, you might end up back at Watermill."

"No, Vlad, I don't need it to steal a car. It's really to hang... oh, just forget it."

Victor abandoned the hammer idea. Plus, the vintage clock was a gift from Ms. Sterling, so he felt guilty destroying it. She'd said it once belonged to her husband.

"If God sends you to hell when you die, the devil will lock you in a room stacked floor to ceiling with alarm clocks," James joked. "That'll be your punishment! And he'll give you books to read but all of the pages will be ripped out."

The former teacher despised damaged books. Coffee stains, ripped pages and gum stuck in-between chapters became the norm at the prison library, and without money to replace the materials, important passages of literature were lost forever to the inmates.

Victor found his new job at the pharmacy more fulfilling. Ms. Sterling had made him a fair and unusual offer: a steady paycheck with reasonable hours if he agreed to evening tea on the front porch each day after closing. He hadn't done much talking during his stint behind bars and missed the company of a friend, so he accepted the offer. Plus, the gig had to be better than slaving away in the sweat factory that was the mechanic's shop.

Like prison, life on the outside fell into a neat routine. Victor and James walked two miles each morning from the halfway house in the rural county to the center of town. They'd follow the double-yellow lines on the blacktop and shift left or right for oncoming cars but mostly had the open road to themselves. Victor would periodically check his wrist watch along the way to make sure he wasn't late. The gears in the old timepiece sprung back to life after he replaced the battery. The second hand ticked with precision.

Some days, rain pounded them both from all angles, even sideways during summer storms. The sharp droplets stung Victor's face and soaked his jeans; he'd change his wet socks at work. On winter mornings, he retreated into his puffy coat for protection from the freeze gnawing at his fingertips, cheeks and nose. The blinding sun bounced off the fresh snow and forced him to shield his eyes. Occasionally, he'd take a break to massage his arthritic knees and stretch his legs before forging forward with his spirit guide by his side.

"Morning, Victor," Patrick Murphy said as he unlocked the front door to the post office, a one-room operation housed out of the back of the courthouse. The postmaster's Dublin accent never faded despite living in upstate New York for decades. Murphy, a former priest, quit the clergy and moved to America, specifically the reclusive town of Emerson, to start a new life with his secret lover, who he eventually married. He settled into a post office job and never left.

"How's your wife?" Victor asked. He'd come to respect Murphy, a frequent customer to the pharmacy.

"She's doing great and is starting…"

"Boy, you causin' trouble again?" a portly man shouted from the driver's side window of a black SUV. Victor took offense to the words *boy*, *trouble* and *again*. Despite every urge in his body to lash out, he held his tongue.

"No sir, sheriff. I'm heading to work."

In prison, he used "yes, sir" and "no, sir" when addressing figures of authority and learned that the courtesy defused testy situations.

Sheriff Milton Molar disdained Victor and all of the other ex-cons living in the halfway house. He focused his razor-sharp attention on those he deemed *problematic*, a category that included thieves, out-of-towners and ex-cons. Molar glared at Victor from behind the tinted, bulletproof windows of his unmarked vehicle. Everyone in the county knew it was the sheriff's truck because there was nothing like it for miles. It had sirens and emergency lights tucked behind the grille and on the dashboard. With the flick of a switch, it lit up like a Christmas tree. Several curly antennas climbed out of the roof.

The short, bald and rotund sheriff opened his door and struggled to climb down from his throne behind the steering wheel. He stretched his legs to a metal foot step before hopping to the ground. Behind his back, Molar's deputies called him "Fat Napoleon."

"You better not be loiterin' because it ain't no trouble sendin' you back to Watermill where you belong. I can call up the warden. He'll welcome you with open arms!"

Molar chomped down on the tobacco tucked in the back of his mouth next to his gums. The wad of chew stretched the skin around his jaw. He spit black onto the sidewalk.

"You don't belong here," he said. "You understand that, right?"

Blood rushed to Victor's face. James felt his rage and stepped in to ease the tension.

"He's a bully with empty threats," the spirit guide said. "Don't challenge him and waste energy because nothing good will come of it — let it go."

Without saying a word, Victor turned his back on both the sheriff and postmaster and walked toward the diner across the street. He heard the sheriff shout, "I'm always watchin' you. I got the warden on speed dial!"

Victor ignored the threat and pulled open the glass door to the retro-style restaurant, which was covered in community calendars, church bulletins and a schedule for the high school football team. It was the only shop on the square with neon lights in the window. The diner had become part of Victor's morning routine. The satiating aroma of bacon, bagels and brewing coffee filled the air. A waitress handed him a laminated menu. Ketchup, mustard and mayo stains dotted her apron, which hung from her frame like a pre-school smock.

"The usual or something new?" Donna asked. "Maybe you could sit down and enjoy breakfast instead of rushing off to work."

"You're kind to offer, but I don't want to be late. A blueberry muffin and a tea would be wonderful."

A cigarette dangled between Donna's scarlet lips. A clump of ash fell next to a basket of freshly-baked bread. She brushed it away with her fingers.

"Customers aren't bothered by your smoking?" Victor asked.

"No one's complained about it."

Donna tossed a piece of a chewing gum into her mouth and chomped down while simultaneously puffing on the cigarette.

"You mean no one has complained about it, yet"

She exhaled gray smoke through her nostrils and pointed to her cigarette.

"This relaxes me, and let me tell you something, this is the most stressful job I've ever had."

James raised his eyebrows — "Stressful?"

"Lots of orders to keep track of and complaining customers asking for things — one person wants salad dressing on the side and another doesn't want peanuts in the salad. It's crazy! One fellow made me take back a drink order because he asked for no ice. Don't even get me started about bad tippers."

"Maybe she'd get more tips if she didn't drop cigarette ash in people's food," James said.

It helped that the county health inspector was Donna's brother. He sat at the same table every morning and ate a triple stack of chocolate-chip pancakes soaked in maple syrup with a side of hash browns. The inspector inhaled his breakfast and paid no mind to his sister's cigarette smoke wafting over his food.

The chain-smoking waitress ignored the respiratory plight of her costumers and puffed away. She lifted the cover to the muffin bin, plucked out a blueberry and batted her eyes at Victor.

"Thank you, Donna," he said before checking his watch. "I have to stop by church before work. See you tomorrow!"

The waitress dropped her smile and gave a half-hearted wave. Victor rushed out of the diner and left change on the counter along with a generous tip.

*

Victor whispered his confession even though there was no priest to receive it. It was a private conversation with God in the empty sanctuary. He pressed his nose to his hands, palm-to-palm in prayer, and bowed his head.

"Forgive me for my sins and all I've done to offend you."

A marble altar draped in purple cloth stood before him — a far cry from his makeshift chapel in the secret room underneath the library. A 5-foot long crucifix suspended on a gold chain hung between two columns. The chalices used for mass were housed in a decorative-box. A violet-colored velvet curtain adorned the back of the altar. Victor never attended services. He felt more comfortable being alone in the church. No need to disrupt the serenity of the sanctuary with a noisy choir and nosy parishioners asking questions about his past. Yes — it was better to be alone in the quiet space, a respite from a chaotic world.

"Forgive me for the life I've taken."

James sat next to Victor in the pew. The spirit guide listened to the stillness for any message from above but none came. His prayers were different than Victor's.

"Please, protect and watch over the ones I love. Keep them safe from harm."

James had grown fond of St. George's Church, and it wasn't only because of his namesake. The building's gothic architecture stood out in the colonial town and dwarfed the courthouse and its malfunctioning clock. Its two stone towers bookended a wafer-like window above a set of bronze front doors. The circular window was 20 feet in diameter and showcased the same image of St. George slaying a dragon that was inked on James's upper arm.

"Weeping may endure for a night, but joy cometh in the morning," Victor recited from the Book of Psalms. The words refreshed his soul as they'd done during darker times. Prayer was his most effective weapon against fear.

He checked his watch again. It was time to go. His wrinkly hands ached as he squeezed the wooden pew in front of him. His knees cracked when he bowed. Victor dipped his arthritic fingers into a ceramic bowl filled with holy water. It soothed him, and for the briefest of moments, the pain went away.

Sculptures of the Stations of the Cross peered down on Victor as he walked up the aisle toward the back of the church — seven on the left side of the church and the remaining seven on the right. He admired the detailed artisanship and how each carved piece captured a story of human suffering. Dancing candle flames cast shadows on the stone artwork. He was also struck by the magnificent organ in the choir loft. Its brass pipes climbed toward the steeple. Maybe one day he'd hear its mellifluous sound.

But his attention was broken by a man's shadow

reflected against a side wall. He whipped around to face the person but no one was there. Victor trained his ears on the silence. No sounds. No movement. He was alone. A backdraft blew underneath the bronze doors and echoed through the cavernous space. Maybe his imagination was playing tricks on him.

It was time for work.

CHAPTER 17
ONE DRUNKEN NIGHT

The mute pharmacist cocked his head at the sheriff whose bulging, bright-red face looked like a pimple close to popping.

"Are you listenin' to me, boy?" he demanded. A wad of chewing tobacco in his mouth assonated his S's and soft C's. "I asked you a question and you look at me like I'm talkin' Chinese. You speak English, don't you? I'm only askin' one more time, so don't make me repeat myself. How many times a day do I take these pills?"

Ed's icy stare cracked the faintest of smiles. He'd succeeded in irritating the sheriff. The pharmacist raised his hand ever so slowly and held up four fingers.

"Four times?" Molar asked. "That's a lot of pills to take."

Without breaking eye contact, Ed pointed to the instructions on the side of the plastic bottle. Molar glanced at the fine print but was uninterested in reading medical jargon. He shot the robotic pharmacist an incredulous stare.

"I don't trust you."

He spun around and pointed at Victor, who was stocking cans of beans and tuna fish in the grocery section at the back of the store.

"Don't trust you either! Thank your lucky stars that I'm not in charge of corrections. Otherwise, you'd both be locked up. I'd throw away the key and never let you out. You wouldn't see the light of day for the rest of your lives."

The sheriff slammed $20 on the counter and strutted away like a peacock. He shut the front door with so much force, the bell hanging above the entrance jingled for nearly a minute after he left.

"Maybe we should offer him chocolate the next time he comes in for a prescription," Victor said. "That might brighten his mood."

Ed's upper lip curled into an awkward smile.

The bell above the front door rang again, and Victor, James and Ed held their breaths, worried the sheriff had returned for a revenge tirade, but thankfully, it was the postmaster who strolled into the shop.

Typically loquacious, Patrick Murphy was instead demure and ignored the men. He snuck through the aisles with his head down and stuffed his plastic handbasket with an eclectic assortment of items like greeting cards, pickle jars, and lightbulbs.

"What's he up to?" James asked.

After several minutes of clandestine movements, Murphy finished his shopping and shuffled to the cash register, where the elderly shopkeeper was perched on a stool, completing a newspaper crossword puzzle. She squinted hard at each letter as she penciled in her answers.

"Oh, I didn't see you there," she said in a feeble voice. "My eyes are getting worse and worse every day. How are you doing today, Patrick? You always look so handsome in your uniform."

Murphy blushed but said nothing.

Ms. Sterling leaned in and whispered, "Do you need to resupply?"

The postmaster peered over both shoulders to ensure no one was listening.

"Yes, ma'am," he whispered.

Sterling surreptitiously grabbed a bottle of pinot noir from a hidden drawer behind the counter, slipped the wine into a brown paper bag and passed it to her anxious customer. The exchange happened within seconds and reminded Victor of one of the many drug deals he'd witnessed in prison.

"As always..." The postmaster's voice got lower, and he muttered out of the corner of his mouth. "Thank you for your discretion."

Murphy's cheeks turned red, and he darted out of the pharmacy. It was a ritual he repeated every Wednesday after his shift.

"Why doesn't he buy wine at the liquor store?" Victor asked Sterling. "That would seem like a better alternative than the charade that happens here."

The old woman eased into a rocking chair in the corner of the shop and wrapped herself in a navy blanket. James thought Sterling looked like a monk.

"Murphy's wife disdains alcohol and believes it's the drink of the devil," she explained. "Patrick loves her, so when they're together, he abides by her wishes. But he's also a wine connoisseur and appreciates a good spirit every now and then. If he bought his bottle at the liquor store, then one of the town gossips would blow his cover. That's why he buys it here."

"En vino veritas," Victor said, reviving his forgotten Latin from his school days.

As Sterling and Victor chatted, James caught his own reflection in a mirror that was part of the rotating display case for cheap reading glasses. He stared back at what should have been a 43-year-old man. Instead, he saw the same kid who'd walked across the bridge all those years ago: dirty-blond hair; hazel eyes; unblemished skin; a pointy nose; lanky arms; a slightly crooked smile and pearly white teeth.

"You've got chicklets in your mouth," his brother would tease. Will also poked fun at the tattoo plastered on James's upper arm.

"Are you joining a biker game or applying for a job as a bouncer?"

James took his brother's playful mocking in stride and returned the verbal jabs. The tit-for-tat was part of their relationship, and they relished how far they could push the insults, each more audacious than the last.

In death, James's spiritual growth had far exceeded anything he could've imagined. A supreme knowledge had been bestowed upon him, a form of enlightenment, and he wanted to impart that wisdom on others, especially Victor. However, he recognized it wasn't his right to share. Victor had to decipher his own life lessons, and there was still so much more to do.

"You've been working hard all day," Sterling said. She used her wooden cane to point at the refrigerator stocked with cold sodas, teas and flavored waters. "Would either of you like something to drink?"

"I'm fine, thank you," Victor said.

Ed was busy counting pills and shook his head no.

"What about a beer?" Sterling asked with a friendly smile.

Victor squeezed his knees with both hands. His tightened grip left finger imprints on his jeans.

"You're certainly full of surprises, Ms. Sterling, but the truth is I don't deserve one." While the idea of drinking a cold beer was refreshing, guilt crushed the temptation. "After what I've done, I shouldn't be allowed anywhere near alcohol for the rest of my life, however long I've got left."

Sterling fidgeted with her fingers. An uncomfortable silence lingered until it was broken by a cluster of wind chimes hanging on the front porch.

"What happened, my dear?" she asked.

It'd been four years since Victor first walked into the pharmacy and drank tea with Sterling on the front porch, and in all that time, she'd never asked him about his past. There were prods here and there but never a direct question.

Victor had avoided sharing his story with anyone, not even his lawyer, who'd advised him not to testify at trial. That meant he never got the chance to explain his actions to the jury. His embarrassed family and enraged wife didn't ask what happened that night. They were too paralyzed by shock and raw anger. Sharing the past with fellow inmates was a bad idea because his survival in prison was predicated on remaining invisible. He interacted with as few prisoners and guards as possible, and when he did, he avoided talking about anything personal, including the crash. The less they knew about his crime, the better. No need to provide ammunition for blackmail. He'd heard stories of inmates threatening to ruin appeals by releasing damaging details and concocting fallacious tales with enough accurate information to sound true. Prison was replete with swindlers, manipulators and snitches who'd sell their own mothers if it benefited them. Victor was unsure how he could be blackmailed but was confident someone would find a way, so his solution was to avoid the topic altogether.

"You should tell her," James urged, curious to hear Victor's side of the story. While he'd long forgiven him, the spirit guide's limited memory of what happened on the old stone bridge consisted only of bright headlights and a car barreling toward him. "It might feel good to talk."

The former teacher took a deep breath through his nostrils and propped himself up on the counter. He looked down at his sneakers, a present from Sterling when he first started working at the pharmacy. She told him his older sneakers wouldn't do and that he needed something more comfortable and presentable if he was to help customers. Sterling had shown him kindness in more ways than one. She deserved to know.

"Twenty years ago, I killed a young man named James St. George because I was driving drunk."

Ed put down his pill bottle and leaned in for a listen. He too wanted to hear Victor's tale.

"There was no reason to drink so much. I had a half-dozen beers plus shots of whiskey. I don't remember much, but it all started with a birthday party for a group of college girls. I bought a round for the table. One of them had red hair. Tara?

Alicia? I can't remember her name. She and her girlfriends probably thought I was such a creep."

He squeezed the crown of his nose like he was trying to suppress a headache. Sterling rocked back and forth in her chair and listened attentively without saying a word.

"The school year had ended, and I'd finished grading final exams. My wife went to her parents for the weekend, so I thought a drink at the bar was my reward for a hard day's work. I was such an arrogant prick." He shook his head in disgust. "My usual spot was The Dragon's Den, but that night I went to the tavern on the square."

James froze. If Victor had gone to The Dragon's Den instead of the other bar, then maybe the crash never would've happened, and he'd still be alive. There was no way James would've allowed a drunken Victor to leave the bar and drive his car.

"I would've confiscated your keys if I saw you were wasted," James said.

Like an adoring grandmother, Sterling smiled in the direction of the spirit guide, who was stunned that she seemed to recognize him. Unsure how to respond, he forced an awkward smile.

"I don't know how long I stayed because it's a giant blur, but when I finally stumbled out of the bar and fell onto the ground, no one rushed over to help," Victor continued. "I threw up into a bed of hydrangeas. My vomit covered the plants. My head pounded in pain.

"I remember seeing a bearded man leaning up against a stone statue of a Chinese dragon guarding the bar's entrance. The stranger's hair was stringy and long. He exhaled a whirl of cigar smoke in my direction. His eyebrows arched high. His nose was pointed like a witch's. His charcoal eyes glared with delight. I was his evening entertainment."

"Did he say anything?" Ed asked, breaking his decades-long silence.

Victor, James and Sterling whipped their heads in toward the lurch-like pharmacist. His voice was deep, yet soft and gentle — not what they expected from a man who'd murdered his father with a shotgun.

"Ed?" Sterling said. She sat up in her rocking chair, but he ignored the shopkeeper and repeated his question. "Did the man say anything?"

"Um... ah... he... um... no," Victor said, struggling to regain his place in the story. "He... ah... didn't... say anything. He only pointed. His eyes glowed behind the gray smoke. I was embarrassed and stumbled toward my car in the parking lot. When I turned the key, the engine growled, so I revved it louder and louder. I think I was trying to make up for my graceless exit from the bar. Maybe someone would be impressed with my sports car. Instead, a couple walking hand-in-hand on the sidewalk shot me a dirty look. The bearded man continued laughing in-between puffs. I even smelled his cigar inside my car. He enraged me."

Sterling scratched her head and interrupted Victor's story.

"Why not stop there and go home?"

"I was invincible. Nothing could stop me. At least, that's how I felt at the time."

"None of us are indestructible," she said.

Victor nodded in agreement and swallowed hard.

"I know that now, but back then, I thought I was."

"What happened next?" James asked.

"It was too early to go home, and I needed to sober up, so I decided to race around town to show off my wheels. The most logical thing to do, right? My tires burned hot when I seared figure eights into the pavement. Smoke as thick as that stranger's cigar climbed into the sky from the treads.

"I shot down Main Street like a bat out of hell. A few folks tried to warn me that I was driving too fast, but I scoffed at them. I remember one woman yelled 'SLOW DOWN' and 'YOU'RE AN IDIOT.' Like the couple on the sidewalk, I thought she was jealous.

"The old stone bridge arches at the center like a ramp. If I gained enough momentum, I thought I could take the car airborne. My foot slammed the accelerator to the floor, and I shifted into fifth gear."

Victor flattened his hand and moved it forward to show his trajectory.

"But when I hit the bridge, the car bottomed out. The bumper scraped the pavement, and I lost control. Sparks went everywhere. The tires screeched, and I…"

He stopped his story to wipe away tears.

"I didn't know what I'd hit. I thought I'd ricocheted off a light post before crashing. My car crumpled. Blood dripped onto my lips from a gash in my forehead. The airbag sucker-punched me and broke my nose.

"The paramedics' voices sounded muffled in my drunken haze. I tried to speak but couldn't say anything coherent. My head felt like someone had used a jackhammer to chisel away pieces of my skull. I should have died. Instead, I walked away with cuts, bruises and a few broken bones. Somehow, I got out of the car on my own. A paramedic who saw me wandering on the bridge told her partner, 'He's drunk out of his mind.' I guess I reeked of booze."

Sterling fixated on Victor's pained expressions.

"When I saw the damage to my car, I went berserk. The engine was exposed. The front grill was smashed. Shattered glass was everywhere. My first reaction was to blame someone else. I yelled at two officers who tried to restrain me. 'Get off of me! Who did this to my car?' I had no clue I was the jackass who caused the damage.

"A burly cop with tattoos on his forearms locked me in a bear hug while his partner snapped on handcuffs. They ignored my temper tantrum and carried me to the cruiser. One of them whispered in my ear, 'You did this, asshole. You killed someone. Do you still care about your fucking car?' I went limp and wished I was dead."

James couldn't take much more and left the pharmacy in a hurry. He felt Sterling's eyes follow him. The spirit guide walked into the middle of the street and stared up at the vast sky. A few stars had peaked before sunset and sparkled through the passing clouds. He wondered if they were the same ones he'd spotted overhead the night he was killed. He wondered if anyone was listening to his pleas for help. He wondered if he'd ever see Lily again.

CHAPTER 18
BRAWLING

The shrill ring from the rotary phone mounted to the wall forced Victor to cover his ears. It was a miracle the relic still worked. He'd pleaded with Ms. Sterling to let him install a newer cordless phone, but she balked.

"If it ain't broke, why fix it?" she said.

"That thing must be as old as her," James said.

The spirit guide swore he saw Ms. Sterling arch her eyebrows at the caustic barb.

Did she hear me?

James noticed she was reacting more to his presence and wondered if she was sensitive to his energy. But as soon as it appeared that she'd recognized him, the nonagenarian would look away and focus her attention on something else. Maybe it was his imagination.

While Ms. Sterling's mental capacity remained strong, her body was slowing down. She shuffled around the pharmacy with measured caution, always relying on her cane for support, as Jose had done. When she wasn't up and about, she spent her time in the rocking chair, where she crocheted and napped. She only got up when the postmaster came in for his *special purchase*. Otherwise, she entrusted Victor with the responsibility of running the shop, overseeing the cash register and keeping the books. He tracked inventory, managed receipts and placed orders — new skills for the former teacher.

"It's for you." Ms. Sterling pointed to the phone. "He won't give his name but says it's urgent."

"Did he say what he wants?"

Victor had never received a phone call at work. She shook her head.

"He would only tell me that it was *important* and that he *needed* to speak with you."

Victor hoisted himself up from his knees. He'd been restocking shelves; this time it was greeting cards. The arthritis was getting worse, and his joints ached. He grabbed the phone and listened through the earpiece for several seconds before speaking.

"Hello? Who's this?"

"Glad...you... answered," said a raspy voice on the other end. His roommate Gumby was struggling to catch his breath. "I... need... help." His hacking phlegmy cough interrupted his talking. "When... can... you... (more coughing)... come back to... the apartment?"

The chain-smoking ex-car thief already had trouble breathing, but he sounded worse than ever. Smoking two packs a day didn't help. The mere act of walking up the stairs had become an aerobics test for a crook once known for his acrobatic abilities.

"What's happened?" Victor asked. His words

were laced with concern. "Is everything okay?"

He pressed the phone to his ear and listened to his roommate, whom he barely spoke to or even saw. Both men kept to themselves inside the halfway house. James had an eerie feeling that Gumby was up to something.

"Can't... say... on... phone."

"Are you sick? Should I call a doctor?" Victor checked his watch. "I'm almost done with work at the pharmacy. I can be home soon."

Sterling interrupted from the rocking chair.

"If it's important, don't waste time. Go home now. Work can wait until tomorrow. Ed will close up shop when he finishes in the pharmacy."

Victor was reluctant to take advantage of Sterling's generosity but decided to accept her offer. Something was wrong. He could sense it.

"Thank you, Ms. Sterling. That's very kind of you. I promise to work late next week to make up for it."

Gumby's muffled voice eked through the phone.

"Need... help. Come... home... please."

James was suspicious and feared this vague request might be some kind of trap. A cold shiver rippled through his core.

"I'll be back to the apartment in fifteen minutes," he told his roommate.

"Maybe we shouldn't go," James said. He clenched his jaw. "Stay here and finish up."

More often than not, Victor listened to his de-facto conscience, but this time he disregarded his spirit guide's direction, grabbed his coat hanging on a chair next to the rotary phone and rushed out of the store.

"Good Night, Ms. Sterling," he said. "I'll see you

in the morning."

*

The door to the apartment opened into a world of stale darkness. Victor pressed his hand to the wall and felt for the light switch, but while dragging his fingers across the crinkled, peeling wallpaper, he ripped his palm on the sharp head of a lonely nail. He cried out and winced in pain. Blood poured out of the wound as if from a leaky faucet. He pulled down the cuff of his shirt and used it to compress the gash.

It was too dark to see if he'd splattered blood across the wall. Not that it mattered much. The dank, dreary and dilapidated halfway house was falling apart and looked like it'd come from the pages of a horror novel. Cobwebs covered the furniture. The few working lightbulbs in the apartment emitted faint, yellowish glows. In many ways, it wasn't much of an improvement from his prison cell.

Victor blindly reached across the coffee table and searched for anything that could stop the bleeding. An opened box of cereal. A butter knife. A rag that smelled like gasoline. It would have to do. He wrapped the cloth around his left hand several times and tightened it. Then, he grabbed the dull butter knife with his uninjured hand, whipped it front of his body like a swordsman and delved deeper into the darkness. He didn't know why he'd picked up the knife but felt like he needed it.

"Gumby?" he whispered. "Are you there?"

The floor boards creaked as Victor and his spirit guide moved toward the bedrooms. Thick clouds obfuscating the moon shifted to allow a sliver of silver light to pour into the hallway and illuminate a pathway to Gumby's bedroom. His door was closed. Victor pressed his ear to the splintered wood. No movement. Only eerie quiet. He relaxed from his stealth position but continued clutching the butter knife, unsure of what lurked on the other side. He held his breath and used the butt of the knife to knock three times.

"Gumby?" Victor asked again. This time, his voice was louder and more authoritative. Still, James detected a hint of fear. "Are you in there?"

"He's inside the room," James said. The spirit guide's nervousness worsened, and the pit in his stomach tightened into a knot.

Victor squeezed the doorknob with his wounded hand — blood seeped through the rag — but before he could turn, a muffled voice on the other side yelled back.

I'm here," Gumby said, garbling his words. "Alone?"

"Yes." Victor cleared his throat. "Can I come in?"

"Only if you're alone."

Victor tried to push open the warped door, but it wouldn't budge, so he used his shoulder. After three shoves, it finally swung open.

The space was mostly empty except for a bed and nightstand. A solitary lightbulb dangled from a broken fixture above a bare mattress. The ex-car thief was lying down with his back propped up against the backboard. He was decked out in denim — jeans and a baggy jacket covered his diminutive frame. Lizard cowboy boots adorned twiggy legs.

When he clicked his heels, bits of dirt unhinged from the soles. He used his tongue to maneuver a toothpick from the left side of his mouth to the right.

"I gather you're contemplating why I called you," he said.

His speech wasn't frantic like on the telephone. Empty beer cans surrounded his skinny body. He chugged what was left in one can before crunching the aluminum and tossing it against the wall. It landed with a tinny thud. The backwash of beer spilled onto the floor. Gumby burped.

"He's drunk — don't waste your time," James said.

"I called you here to discuss a business opportunity," Gumby said.

Victor crossed his arms.

"Listen, I don't need to hear about any business propositions," he said sharply. "I'm working at the pharmacy and saving money. I left that job and rushed over because I thought you needed my help."

"Hear me out and listen to what I've got to say."

Gumby moved his legs to reveal what he'd been concealing: two bricks of cocaine; several dozen small bags stuffed with marijuana; a clear bag filled with 100 white pills; a roll of cash wrapped in a rubber band; a 12-inch hunting knife and a sawed-off double-barrel shotgun.

"Oh my God," James said.

Victor's feet froze to the ground. His hands trembled.

"How did you get all of this?" he asked.

"No need for an inquisition," the ex-con spat back as he plucked out the toothpick and flicked it to the ground. It landed next to the crumpled beer cans. "All you need to know is that it's part of a promising business venture. Of course, the goods are all on loan. I don't have the capital to make this kind of purchase, but when I sell the drugs, I'll make a pretty profit. Capitalism at its finest — don't you love it!"

Gumby threw his spaghetti arms up in victory, but James thought the celebration premature. The once notorious thief was now a drug kingpin, or at least trying to become one.

"You mean illegal capitalism that can land you back in prison," Victor responded. "I didn't know it was possible to be both insane and a complete idiot. You'll get caught, and when they nab you, forget parole. You'll die at Watermill. The warden will make sure of that."

"You're making some serious assumptions, amigo. Might I enumerate my rebuttal?"

Despite his cartoonish nickname and country bumpkin ways, Gumby had an impressive vocabulary and used it to confuse his adversaries during shady deals. His verbal assault would befuddle opponents, and more often than not, the tactic worked. By the time the other party realized they'd been swindled, Gumby was long gone.

The skinny ex-con counted off his fingers as he made his points.

"First, I won't get caught because I'm a consummate professional who pays the utmost attention to detail. Ineptitude is inexcusable. My previous incarceration stemmed from a jailhouse snitch seeking quid pro quo for a reduced sentence. I'm wiser now and know the pitfalls of the game. Remember what Oscar Wilde said, 'Experience is the name we give ourselves.' Wasn't he a writer or something?"

Victor rolled his eyes and recoiled from the stench of alcohol. Gumby reeked of booze.

"Secondly, no one would suspect an old thief like me to get back on the streets. Age is my camouflage, and therefore my greatest asset.

"Lastly, I'll have your assistance. Two minds are better than one. Batman had Robin. The Lone Ranger had Tonto. Holmes had Watson. I have Victor Young! Old and Young working together! Kind of catchy, wouldn't you say? We'll make more money than you've ever imagined, more than whatever that hag at the pharmacy is paying you, enough money to get out of this shithole."

"You should walk away," James said. "There's no reason to get involved in any of this."

Victor's conscience was right, yet he was paralyzed by violent thoughts racing through his mind. He wanted to grab the shotgun from the mattress and fire both barrels into Gumby's chest — time to put the old crook out to pasture. He'd be doing the world a favor. Victor planned it out in his head; he could flee to Canada before anyone knew what had happened. His roommates wouldn't venture into Gumby's bedroom for days, so he'd have a head start.

Victor surprised himself at how quickly his frustration had morphed into rage. He thought he'd learned how to control his anger. Still, Gumby deserved to be punished for jeopardizing the well-being of everyone in the halfway house.

"What you do here will affect everything you've worked so hard to achieve," James said. "Why jeopardize all of your progress? Don't do anything stupid!"

Victor's appetite for violence lessoned following

James's insistence and his anger faded almost as quickly as it had appeared. He felt calmer.

"Why would I help you, Gumby? I'm no drug dealer. Yes, I spent time in prison for killing someone but that doesn't make me a street thug." He looked directly into the eyes of the denim-clad skeleton on the bed. "I want nothing to do with this!"

Gumby leapt to his feet and soared through the air like a gymnast. The heels of his boots slammed against the floor and left an indentation in the wood. A stern glare replaced his shiny smile.

"My friend, you're more like me than you know." Gumby's beady eyes darkened. "No one makes it out of Watermill unscathed unless they're mentally tough, and you made it out just fine. Like me, you have an innate survival skill, and you're the only person in this shitty apartment with the smarts to help me earn a return on my investment."

Gumby stood on his tiptoes and pushed his face close to Victor's, so that they were nose-to-nose. His tobacco and beer breath were overbearing. Black nose hairs danced when he spoke.

"We can make cash — lots of it! Why wouldn't you want to make money? The way I see it, you're either with me or against me."

James jumped between the two and forced Gumby to stumble back. The ex-con was startled by his sudden lack of balance.

"We're not doing anything together," Victor reiterated. "You're on your own."

Gumby coughed up a single laugh, which is all that his barely-functioning lungs would allow. He didn't know it yet, but he was dying of lung cancer. He spat black saliva onto the bedroom floor and narrowly missed Victor's foot.

"What you can't seem to ascertain is that you have don't have a choice in this matter," he growled.

Gumby straightened the lapels on his denim jacket and smiled.

"What you see on this bed is only a small portion of what I've purchased. There's product hidden all across this apartment, the garage downstairs and even in the woods surrounding the gas station."

He spread his arms wide like wings.

"I hid drugs underneath floor boards and also in the attic. Maybe I even stashed something at your pharmacy. No one would ever expect Sterling Pharmacy to be a drug house of the recreational variety. That would be a sad turn of events for such a cornerstone of this community."

Victors face turned red. He tightened his knuckles and dug his fingernails into his palms. James grabbed the back of his shirt and tried to pull him back, but he wouldn't budge.

"Don't fight him," the spirit guide urged. "That's what he wants."

Gumby continued his rant.

"All it takes is one phone call to the sheriff to pique his interest. A cursory search of this apartment would send all of us all back to Watermill. A search of the pharmacy would also cause trouble for Ms. Sterling too. Oh, what the detectives might find! Who would suspect the elderly proprietor of a neighborhood institution would be linked to a narcotics operation?"

Victor's fist made a direct connection with Gumby's crooked nose. The bones and cartilage crunched from the blow and spewed crimson across the wallpaper. The diminutive man winced in pain and fell backwards onto the bed, accidentally swallowing his chewing tobacco. He wailed in agony again, this time from the unsheathed hunting knife on the mattress that jammed into his hamstring. Blood poured out of the back of his leg. Gumby grimaced as he yanked out the blade and threw the bloody weapon across the room like a boomerang. The wannabe kingpin moaned and nursed his injuries.

"We need to leave right now!" James yelled.

His words resonated more resolutely than ever before. To Victor, it sounded like another person was in the room. He even turned and looked for the source of the voice, but no one was there.

"Yes," Victor said. "It's time go."

CHAPTER 19
THE WISE OLD OWL

Fog quieted the noisy world. Rain drops ricocheted off James's nose. The pattering on his skin soothed him, and panic gave way to calm. He'd experienced the same change in emotions during his first night in prison, when God dropped him in the middle of a hostile world without warning. At the time, he found solace in the bright stars shining through the bars on the window. If only he could reach out and grab them now, then maybe he could get back to heaven.

James watched Victor cut through the dense haze and bolt toward a cabbie fueling up his taxi at the gas pumps. The only light came from a crooked lamppost. Many cars had accidentally reversed into the post over the years and bent it a few additional degrees with each subsequent hit. Somehow, it remained standing and was one of the few working streetlights along Old Country Way.

"Can you take me to the church on the square?" Victor asked the driver.

His words were rushed. The cabbie studied the customer's twitching face before considering the unusual, late-night request. As long as Victor paid in cash, then no questions asked.

"Twenty bucks," the cabbie said. "That's the night rate. If you got a problem with the price, then call someone else."

The driver unhinged the nozzle from his beat-up boat of a sedan and closed the broken flap to his tank, which shut unevenly against the body of the car. Gasoline spilled onto the blacktop as he transferred the hose back to the pump — a dangerous maneuver for a man with a lit cigarette hanging from his bottom lip. Victor saw it too and froze as if any motion might cause a piece of hot ash to drift into the fuel collecting by their feet. An explosion would be epic, but the cabbie didn't seem to care.

While the top of his head was bald, he had enough hair to make a ponytail. He puffed on his cigarette and exhaled through his nostrils, shooting two streams of tobacco smoke into the fog. The red glow from his cigarette illuminated wild, fiendish eyes — more animal than human.

"I have the cash… somewhere in my pocket," Victor said. He dug deep into his wrinkled jeans, pulled out a crumpled twenty-dollar bill and forced it into the man's hairy fist. As if to test its authenticity, the cabbie pressed the money in-between his fingers and waved it in the air. He then flicked what was left of his cigarette to the pavement, mere feet from the spilled fuel, and stamped out the butt with his scuffed-up boot. Bits of smoldered ash burned in the haze.

"Let's go," he said coldly.

"Thank you — as fast as you can."

"At your service," the cabbie replied with a tinge of sarcasm.

He opened the backdoor and bowed like a butler. "Azrael Taxi" was printed in white lettering along the black driver side door. The car's original yellow color appeared through scratches along the bumpers and doors. James jumped into the back seat with Victor.

No one spoke during the foggy journey into town. A lingering melancholy filled the car. Victor's eyebrows felt heavy. His shoulders slumped. A throbbing pain in his head grew to a walnut's size. He was too exhausted to speak and rested his head against the window, staring outside at the soupy world. Visibility was pour. The cabbie couldn't see more than 20 feet ahead. The car's high beams bounced off the fog and blinded the driver.

"It's no use," he grumbled and switched the running lights to low beams.

The jalopy rolled across the old stone bridge. Its tires squeaked on the wet, uneven stones. It was as if the slick roadway was speaking to them. James thought he heard the whispers say *stay away*.

The river flowing underneath looked like an eerie lagoon. No signs of life except for cattails and water lilies. Algae and moss covered the sides of the bridge.

One of the headlights on the taxi burned out, leaving only a solitary beam to light the path.

"Lamp's gone," the cabbie said. "No reason to worry. I'll get you there in one piece."

The driver slowed to a crawl in the darkness. Victor continued gazing out of the window.

"Are you okay?" James asked.

No response. He couldn't see Victor's face but

felt his pain. The former teacher remained quiet for the remainder of the trip.

*

The cab came to an abrupt stop in front of stone steps leading to the church's entrance. Victor's body jolted forward in the back of the taxi, and he hit his head on the driver's headrest. The brakes shrieked and forced him to cover his ears.

"Not the smoothest of parking jobs," James said.

He rolled his eyes and glanced up at the impressive, steeples shrouded in mist and understood why Victor liked coming here; there was no other architecture like it in the entire county, and it beat praying in the secret room underneath the library. Beams of light shot through circular, stained-glass windows embedded in the brass doors and illuminated the steady rainfall.

Without uttering a word, Victor opened the taxi door, jumped out of the back seat and vanished into the mist. He moved so quickly, James had to scramble out of the car to keep pace.

Through his rearview mirror, the cabbie watched the men bolt away. His eyes followed their angled reflections until they disappeared up the steps. He tucked Victor's money into a red bag filled with cash and stashed it in the glove box. The smoke from his cigarette wafted toward the digital clock on the dashboard. The numbers radiated a blueish hue. Time to find the next fare. The engine chugged, and the taxi vanished into the rainy night, a solitary headlamp lighting the way.

James watched the car putt away. He was happy to

see it go and could have sworn the cabbie glared at him when he hopped out of the back seat. Good riddance.

As for Victor, he was nowhere to be found. The spirit guide thought he saw him dart up the stairs toward the beams of light, but when he reached the bronze doors, Victor was gone.

"Victor!"

Quietness spawned dread, and panic set in.

"Are you there?" James shouted. "Can you hear me?"

But instead of Victor's voice, James was greeted with three successive hoots. The noises echoed from a soaring sycamore in the cemetery adjacent to the church. The tree's branchy limbs protruded in all directions as if warning intruders to stay away. Its leaves rustled in the wind. Rain droplets plopped into puddles pooling around the tree trunk and echoed in the night.

James walked down the slippery steps and ventured into the mushy, cemetery grass. He cocked his head and scoured the branches for the owl, but it was too foggy. The rain stung his eyes.

"You're mocking me, aren't you?" he shouted toward the sky.

The robust sycamore provided a canopy to parishioners enjoying their eternal rest. The neglected graveyard was home to 200 souls. Most of the lopsided headstones were faded. Some had names without dates, while others had dates without names. A few of the tombstones had crumbled. Poor parishioners had flat stones flush with the earth. Overgrowth covered the markers. James was unaware he was standing atop a plot until his foot stepped on a smooth rock. He felt guilty and jumped off the grave. Wealthier parishioners had built towering monuments that included ornate pillars made of limestone, marble and granite. One deceased church-goer had commissioned a stone replica of himself, including a long beard, monocle and pet parrot on his right shoulder. Another gravestone had a chiseled image of a rippling American flag. Intricate headstones dotted the cemetery, but one in particular stood out among the rest.

The onyx obelisk pointed directly to heaven. The 12-foot tall pillar glimmered even in the darkness. James wiped away rain drops collecting along the marker's inscription. The letter "K" was featured prominently above the year of death, 1987. A phoenix carved into the base of the obelisk rose from a pile of ashes and stretched its wings in flight. He remembered the magical bird's symbolic representation of rebirth and renewal from his Shakespeare class. James's eyes followed the obsidian headstone upward, where he found two perfectly circular, yellow eyes staring back at him.

"You've been watching me this entire time, haven't you?"

The owl had perched itself atop the pyramidal stone pillar, where it studied the spirit guide standing below. Its golden eyes floated in the night. If only the nocturnal creature could talk and spills its secrets.

"I know you know where he is."

The bird rotated its head but didn't blink. Instead, it fixed its gaze on James, who widened his eyes in frustration to mimic the owl. The bird reciprocated by opening its smallish beak as if to hoot but made no sounds. It ruffled its wet feathers and brushed off a frigid breeze that was stripping leaves off branches. But even the wind couldn't shake the resolute creature clinging to the top of the obelisk.

James picked up a pebble, rubbed off the dirt with his fingers and considered chucking it at the wise old owl but decided against it. He knew it was wrong. No reason to take his anger out on the innocent bird.

"I need your help," he admitted.

The owl straightened its head as if it understood, and then took flight. Its wing span was large for a petite bird. It soared high above the sycamore and made a full rotation, diving in and out of the fog, before passing within a few feet of James's head. The owl landed on a streetlamp near the stone steps, and sitting on the curb directly underneath the vaporous light, was Victor.

"Victor!" James yelled.

The spirit guide dodged headstones like a running back and darted out of the cemetery.

"Where've you been?" he shouted with relief. "I've been looking all over for you."

Victor buried his hands deep into his pockets and dropped his head and shoulders. His tears mixed with the rainwater.

"What a wasted life," he muttered. "Look at me. I'm an ex-con being black-mailed by an ex-con, and all this time, I've been trying to make things right."

James put his arm around his friend.

"You repented and sought forgiveness," he said. "You made good on your promise to change, and over time, you showed God that you're making a difference. Look at all the good you've done at the pharmacy. He'll forgive you just like I did. Life's too short to wallow in sadness."

"I'm sorry, James," Victor said. "From the bottom of my heart, I'm sorry for everything."

In front of a church with which he shared a name, James hugged his killer. A bond forged in violence linked their souls. The spirit guide realized at that moment he'd spent more time with Victor than any other person, more than with his parents, brother or even Lily.

Victor stopped shuddering and listened to the wind. He could have sworn he heard a voice, someone speaking to him, a faint whisper in the distance. The owl watched both men rise from the curb and climb the limestone steps. When they reached the top, Victor grabbed the cylindrical door handles shaped like scrolls and pulled, but they wouldn't budge. He banged hard on the locked metal doors with his fists, but no one came. He and James stood on their tiptoes and peered through the windows, and what they saw overwhelmed them.

A sea of candles in nearly every square inch of the sanctuary filled the space with radiance. They lined the slate floors, the wooden pews and even the statues, including the one of Jesus Christ wearing a crown of thorns. In both of his open palms were candles with three wicks. The smaller flames combined to form a larger one.

The plethora of light beat back the darkness. Chandeliers above the pews burned brightly, as did a row of torches lining the altar. A sculpture of St. George slaying a dragon sat at the front of the church. The beast's mouth was filled with a dozen smaller candles, which gave the illusion of a fire-breathing monster.

Various saints depicted in the stained-glass

windows sprang to life. They shined greens, blues, purples, pinks and reds as they peered down on the fiery church. Victor and James squinted in awe at the ineffable glow. Their faces warmed from the thousands of burning candles. Still, they couldn't stop staring at the mesmerizing beauty. Victor scanned the church for a priest or nun, but the holy space was deserted.

"Do you feel the heat from the flames too?" James asked.

He flattened his face to the glass, which warmed his cheeks and nose. For the first time in decades, the spirit guide felt alive. Memories flooded back almost instantaneously: the blazing fireplace at his parent's home; a hot shower; the campfire he and his friends built during their hikes; a sweltering summer day; the ride in his brother's convertible.

But the warming quickly dissipated and gave way to cool air. James's fingertips on the glass felt a chill. He couldn't understand why the temperature was changing, because the candles inside the church continued to burn. His concentration was interrupted by a thick haze materializing on the other side of the doors like water particles clinging together. The vapor obscured his view of the church. White light surrounded a woman's face. He didn't see her smile at first because there was so much smoke. Her blond hair, bright blue eyes and beaming grin radiated pure love just as they always had. His heart skipped a beat.

"Lily?"

Her smile widened to match his. She didn't speak. Instead, her energy pulsated through his heart, and he was able to read her thoughts.

"Are you okay?" he asked.

He felt a yes.

"Will I see you again?"

Another yes.

"When?"

No response.

"Will you stay with me?"

No.

"Are you happy?"

Yes.

"Do you miss me?"

Yes

"Why did this happen to us?"

No answer.

He lowered his voice and let the words fall from his lips, "You're the love of my life."

He heard a whisper.

I love you too.

James pushed his face to the glass to get closer.

"There's so much I have to tell you, so much has happened since I died. I went to heaven and met Grandpa and God. Then, God asked me to be a spirit guide."

Lily smiled and listened as he spoke. She'd always loved hearing him tell stories, even when he rambled and wasn't making any sense. His animated expressions were full of life. She listened to his heart.

I've always been with you.

He didn't see the handprint on the glass at first — a woman's left hand. Lily had a distinctive heart line, stretching her index finger to her pinky. He'd tease her about her lanky fingers.

"You'll scare away all of your patients when you become a nurse, but at least you'll be a hit on Halloween," he'd joke.

Now, James missed those lanky fingers. He matched his hand to the print on the window. If only he could hold her hand again.

Soon but not yet.

CHAPTER 20
GOLDEN DUST FROM HEAVEN

A loud screech followed by a crunch of metal and shattering glass broke James's blissful trance. The jumble of jarring noises jolted him back to reality. Vibrations from the explosion rippled up the limestone steps and reverberated through the church's doors. James felt the pulsating through his hand pressed to the circular glass. He peeled away his fingers. Lily's handprint and smiling face were gone. St. George's was as before, quiet and filled with burning candles.

James opened his mouth to plead for Lily's return but was paralyzed by her sudden absence. He was a voiceless lover in distress. There'd been no time to say goodbye.

"Help! We need help! Please! Someone help us!"

The high-pitched screams echoed from the hazy street below. It was a young woman's voice but not Lily's. James peered into the church one last time to make sure she wasn't still there before he raced down the slippery steps toward the yelling. The stench of charred rubber and spilled diesel filled his nostrils and caused his eyes to tear. He ignored the pungent whiff, and when he reached the bottom of the road, scanned both sides of the street. The screaming continued, but now he also heard a young man's voice.

"We need an ambulance!" he shouted. "Can anyone help us?"

But help was not on its way. The town square was deserted, and the church rectory was dark. James stuck out both of his arms and felt blindly through the fog, unsure of where he was going or what he might find.

For the second time in a night, he lost track of Victor. James had been so engrossed with Lily and had no idea how long he'd been gazing into the church. It could have been minutes or even hours.

"Victor!" James yelled. "Can you hear me?"

No response.

Once again, he'd broken his promise to God and felt ashamed, but there was little time to dwell on his mistake. The girl's panic-laced words were getting louder.

"Is anyone there?" she pleaded. "Please, come quick!"

The fog parted like a curtain when he came upon the crash. James stopped in his tracks as painful memories of his own death flooded back. A mangled black taxi was wrapped around a bent streetlamp. Its overhead light flickered in the rainy darkness, revealing the outlines of three people on the pavement — a young couple hovering over a lifeless body. The teens blocked his view of the injured person's face.

He knew the boy, a local farmhand, who was a regular at the gas station. He'd drive tractors and pickups to get refueled. James always thought the 16-year-old looked cartoonish behind the giant wheel of a backhoe. He usually wore a white T-shirt and muddied boots, but on this night, he was dressed in a yellow collared shirt and khakis. The boy gave mouth-to-mouth to the injured person, whose chest rose and fell with each breath. It didn't appear to be working. The frightened girl kneeling next to him wore a contorted look of terror. She was petite, brown hair, blue eyes, floral dress. She grabbed the victim's hand and felt for a pulse.

"Anything?" the boy asked. "We've got to keep him alive until paramedics arrive."

"It's faint," she said softly.

Tears streamed down her porcelain cheeks. The farmhand switched to chest compressions but still couldn't bring the limp body back to life. Two long legs poked out from underneath the couple. Canvas sneakers pointed in opposite directions, too large to be a woman's feet.

"We can't let him die," the girl cried.

It wasn't clear how anyone could survive the crash. Evidence of the ferocity lay strewn across the street. The driver's side door hung from its hinges to reveal a crushed steering column, damaged dashboard and stuffing poking out from dilapidated leather seats. No airbags. No passengers. No driver. The front grill and hood had folded like cardboard. Smoke from the taxi's engine mixed with the haze. The windshield had shattered on the blacktop. Each fragment reflected a warm tinge from the streetlamp's incandescent light — a colorful mosaic of broken shards. James looked at the driver's side door and spotted the same white lettering he'd seen earlier in the evening: "Azrael Taxi."

He assumed the injured man on the ground was the chain-smoking cabbie but couldn't be certain. The spirit guide crept past the wreckage to get a better view. The teens giving the man aid continued shouting for help, but their pleas fell on deaf ears.

"The car came so fast," the girl said. "I didn't see it."

"Neither did I." The boy's voice quivered. "I didn't hear it until it was a few feet away."

The teen started compressions again and hoped his last-ditch effort would revive the unresponsive man. Sweat dripped down his arms.

"He pushed you out of the way, didn't he?" the girl asked. Her eyes widened. "I saw him do it. He saved you."

The boy stopped compressions and nodded uneasily.

"I don't know how he got to me so fast because the taxi was speeding. When I turned and saw the headlight, I froze, and he shoved me to the sidewalk."

The boy's hands shook uncontrollably and his teeth chattered. He knew that death had come knocking but passed him over for another.

The light drizzle turned into a steadier rainfall, and the pitter-patter of droplets drowned out the girl's teary screams. Gravel, blood and dirt swirled down a storm drain. James looked up at the storm clouds and spotted two yellowish eyes peering down from atop the streetlamp. The watchful owl ruffled its wet feathers in the wind and observed with a distant caution. Once again, James felt betrayed by the voyeuristic bird.

"Go get help," he demanded. "Be useful and do something — don't just sit there!"

He immediately felt guilty for shouting at the bird. The owl blinked, studied James's distressed expression, ignored his orders and glared back in silent defiance.

"Where's Victor?"

The bird rotated his neck toward the unresponsive body in the middle of the street. The teens had stopped trying to resuscitate the man and instead were hugging each other. The steady rain intensified to an all-out downpour, and the stinging droplets pounded them with ferociousness. The owl abandoned their company for cover and swooped underneath the flickering streetlamp before launching into the stormy night. Its outstretched wings revealed a beautiful pattern of white and auburn feathers.

"We've got to get him to the sidewalk or else he'll drown in the gutter," the boy shouted over the fierce winds and thunder. He folded his wet jacket underneath the injured man's head. The water was rising fast. Blood from a gash on his chest washed into the grimy street and turned the rainwater scarlet. Bolts of electricity illuminated the gray sky. The couple pulled the body across the pavement and onto a grassy patch underneath a red rose bud tree. Its purple canopy and elongated branches provided little protection from the weather, but it was better than nothing. James rushed over too and knelt down to get a closer look at the injured man.

Victor's eyes were sealed shut by dirt. His hair was matted down, and he was bleeding from innumerable cuts across his body. There were broken bones, including one protruding from his thigh. His limbs contorted in unnatural directions. James cried out and cradled his friend's head.

"Victor! Can you hear me?"

The farmhand and his date watched with pained stares.

"You're going to be okay. You have to hang on. God's going to help you, and I'm here to protect you."

But the spirit guide feared the end was near. Dread filled his heart. The harsh reality was that there was nothing he could do to save his friend. After guiding him through gangs, drugs, sabotage, beatings, poison, loneliness, isolation and life beyond prison, James had neglected to shield Victor from a gypsy cab outside of a church on rainy night.

If only I hadn't gotten distracted. How could have I been so reckless? How could I have been so foolish?

"His pulse is gone," the sobbing girl said.

She dropped his wrist.

At that moment, the downpour stopped, and the thunder, lightning and stormy clouds gave way to a starry sky. James and the young couple jerked their heads to the heavens for a glimpse of the bizarre transition of weather. The full moon stood out against a black canvas. Millions of tiny lights flanked the glowing sphere.

"The stars are peepholes to heaven," Lily once told him when they were lying on a blanket together at night. "The angels are staring back at us, so when you look at a star, you're looking into their eyes."

James certainly felt as if he was being watched. If

only someone would come down and tell him that everything would be all right. He put his hand on his friend's cold forehead and kissed him on the cheek.

"Look at all of the yellow," the girl said, her voice suddenly filled with excitement.

Scores of fireflies soared out of a cluster of shrubs and looped into a glowing formation like a squadron of planes. There were dozens of glow bugs, some bigger and brighter than others. James hadn't seen anything like it. The bursts of sparkly yellow danced around the tree and sent purple petals spiraling onto Victor's chest. The bugs hovered above his body and blanketed him with golden dust.

"What are they doing?" the boy asked.

"They're guiding his soul to the other side," the spirit guide responded. "It's his time."

An unusually large firefly jumped from Victor's chest and landed on James's shoulder, leaving a trail of sparkling powder in its path. James smelled honeysuckle as he had all those years ago on the old stone bridge. The lightning bug hovered before taking off into the night with the cluster of other bugs. Their combined glow lessened as they climbed into the sky and became specks among the stars.

Victor Young died at 1:00 a.m. on a humid Saturday in July.

CHAPTER 21
THE GIANT BIRCH

Dancing mayflies wrestled in the summer air and zipped and zoomed from tree to tree. Cicadas provided rhythmic sounds to the aerial acrobatics. After tussling underneath the sun, the insects grew tired of their twirling and rested on leaves floating along the crystal-clear water. Most had fallen from dogwood trees lining the banks of the river that twisted through a dense forest.

Unbeknownst to the fatigued bugs, their temporary respite left them vulnerable to the trout lingering below the surface. Following several seconds of stillness, the hungry fish made its move. With one large gulp, it shot toward the jagged leaf and swallowed the insect whole. The remaining mayflies took flight to live another day, while the trout with a satisfied belly wiggled back toward the riverbed. James marveled at how the fish moved with elegant purpose.

But the predator soon became the prey.

A man wearing waders and holding a fishing rod planted his feet into the rocky bottom to balance against a strong current rippling past his knees. An olive-colored fishing hat with a soft brim cast a shadow on his face. His canvas vest sparkled from yellow lures pinned to the fabric. The pockets were stuffed with gear: weights and swivels; spinners; hooks; matches and pliers.

"You're not going to catch any fish by staring at them," he said in a loud whisper.

James watched while standing on a flat rock along the river bank. Its texture and grayish-brown hue reminded him of one of the stones that made up the bridge where he died. He rubbed its smooth surface and felt the past.

The man whipped the fishing line above his head as if he was lassoing a bull. He moved with an artful grace as he cast his feathery lure high into the air among the mayflies. The hooked decoy left a trail of golden dust that floated gently down onto the river. The colorful powder reflected the light like the glistening trout. James watched the effervescent sprinkling come together to form a larger shape. A mysterious, magnetic force pulled the magical particles together, and the bright specks coagulated to make a yellowish-blue rectangle.

"I never did get a chance to take you fly fishing," the man said. "There's so much to see in nature if you pay attention to the omens. The forest, the birds and even the fish speak to you, but if you ignore the signs, then you won't understand their meaning."

The floating shape flashed a bright white before morphing into a living, breathing thing. The blob opened its mouth. Fins grew out of its sides along with eyes, gills and scales. A full-length trout with yellow stripes stretching the length of its body emerged from the colorful mess and swam in circles. The fish born out of dust cut downstream.

James's eyes widened with awe — "How'd you do that?"

The man reeled in his line, removed his canvas hat and smiled.

"I've been waiting for you," the fisherman said.

"Dad?"

James rushed into the water toward his father. The current stopped flowing and the rippling slowed to stillness, allowing him to slice through the river without falling over. When they embraced, James nearly tackled his dad, who dropped his fishing pole, which scared the fish away. He clung to his father's vest like a child afraid to let go. Both had dreamt of this moment, but only as a distant vision buried in the recesses of their broken hearts, uncertain if a reunion would ever come. Prayer, faith and hope brought them together.

"I thought I'd never see you again," James said. "I wish I could've said goodbye."

His father grabbed his shoulder.

"None of that matters now. I've missed you more than you'll ever know."

"Are we in heaven?"

"Yes — we're in my heaven. Like Grandpa, I loved fishing too. He comes to see me, and we take out the rowboat together. There's good catch farther downstream where the river widens. Lately, I've been spending most of my time in shallow water to practice my casting technique."

"Dad, I'm so sorry." James lowered his head and

his voice. "I never should've walked across that bridge. I should've waited or went a different way."

"There's no reason to apologize, because you did nothing wrong and can't be blamed for what happened. You were heading to your pickup and had no control over the man driving that car. It was all part of your destiny."

His father looked like he remembered. Streaks of gray colored his thinning-black hair. Wrinkles hovered underneath his eyes and above his brow. His brilliant eyes radiated a bright blue, a trait James jealously wished he'd inherited.

The last time he saw him was Christmas, when everyone gathered at the family house to celebrate. James was nervous because he'd brought Lily home to meet the family. They'd met previous girlfriends, but Lily was different. He knew the moment he met her that she was his soulmate, the love of his life, and his parents' blessing meant the world to him. Much to his relief, they all loved her.

"I planned to marry Lily and start a family but..." James felt a heavy sadness in his chest. "I thought I had more time."

"Time is the most precious commodity," his father said. "We have to make the best of the time we have because we don't know our endpoint." He kissed his son's forehead. "This was meant to be your journey. It was God's plan, and it was God's plan for me too."

"How do you mean?"

"We all have life lessons. It's the only way our souls can mature. We're constantly being tested and must learn from those experiences, however arduous and painful. Think of a man who lost a leg in war, a child dying of cancer or a woman who loses her sight."

"But how was my death your life lesson?" James asked.

"The death of a child is the worst kind of loss. When I lost you, a piece of me died, because you were part of me. The energy force connecting us was severed, and my world of color dulled and filtered only gray and black."

His father lost his trademark smile.

"The truth is I didn't want to live anymore. Each day was a struggle to survive, but I forged forward because I knew your mother and brother, and ultimately my grandson, needed me. So together, we battled through the pain. It took years for me to return to normalcy, and even then, I was never fully whole. Loss was my life lesson. My soul had to endure the loss of a child."

They embraced once more and squeezed each other tightly.

"It's good to finally have you home."

"I'm so happy to be back, but there's something else," James said. "I failed God. I was supposed to keep Victor safe, and I didn't."

"Why do you think you failed?"

"Victor died."

"Your mission wasn't to keep Victor alive. It was to protect him. You had no control over that taxi, and you couldn't stop Victor from sacrificing his life to save the farmhand. There'll be plenty of time to talk about this later. Right now, there are people waiting to see you, and like me, they've been waiting a long time."

His father pointed toward a meadow filled with a panoply of wildflowers. Pinks, whites, yellows and blues covered the rolling hills. The only tree in the parade of color was a birch that sprouted in the middle of a green field. It stretched nearly 200 feet into the sky, taller than any tree James had ever seen. Its distinctive trunk was a gray, paper-like bark. Its bushy branches hovered among the clouds and provided shade to the people picnicking underneath it.

James's mother, grandfather, brother and sister-in-law lounged on a red-and-white polka-dot blanket where they feasted on turkey and brie sandwiches, pickles, blueberries and strawberries, an array of cheeses and bread and cookies.

"I love chocolate-chip cookies, especially the soft ones," Grandpa said. "You know how to bake them just right."

His sugary chuckle echoed across the valley.

"You're going to spoil your appetite and will have no room left for real food, so stop eating all of the sweets," James's mother scolded.

"I let my stomach guide my food choices, and right now, cookies are what I crave," Grandpa said with a grin.

"Mom, can you pass me another sandwich?" James's brother Will asked.

His mother put two sandwich halves on a ceramic plate and handed it across the blanket.

"Lettuce, mayo, tomato, turkey and cheese — is that okay?"

"Perfect! I'm starving," Will said and chomped into crumbling focaccia barely holding the sandwich together. A slice of cheese lathered in mayonnaise fell onto his jeans. "Why am I so clumsy?" He peeled the cheese from his pants and wrapped it in a napkin.

James's heart burst with excitement. He'd thought of his family every day since he died and often wondered what they were doing and what important milestones he was missing: ice-cream birthday cakes; dad's gourmet cooking; holiday celebrations; weddings; births. Even though God assured him that he'd see his family again, he was skeptical. He wanted to believe but the shock of his own death and the immediate separation from everything he knew left him alone and disconnected. But here they were together again as God had promised. James rushed out of the water and sprinted toward the colossal tree.

"Mom!" he shouted, so loudly he surprised even himself. His sprint turned into a run. James's father watched from the river and laughed with exhilaration. He feared if he didn't get to her fast enough, she might disappear like one of God's swirling visions in the ocean.

"James!" his mother yelled.

She lunged for her youngest child. The moment she dreamt of had finally arrived.

"I've missed you so much," she cried and squeezed her son, kissing him on both cheeks. "I wish I could have protected you."

"There's nothing you could've done, so don't blame yourself."

He recognized the irony of his words after having had the same conversation with his father minutes earlier. He too repeated what his dad had told him.

"None of what happened is your fault."

James grabbed his mother's shoulders and stared into her eyes.

"I'm sorry I never got to say goodbye."

He rubbed his head like he was trying to press

away a headache.

"One moment I was there, and before I knew it, I was gone," he told her. "It happened so fast, and I had no time to get out of the way. After I died, my spirit guide Charlie crossed me over. I met Grandpa, who was fishing in the river. Then, I met God on the beach, who told me…"

"I know," his mother interrupted. "We'll talk about all of that later. What's important now is that we're together. Not even death can break the bonds of love."

"Wait — how do you know?"

She smiled.

"God explained everything to me when I died, but I didn't meet Him on a beach like you. Instead, we met on a shiny, wooden ship surrounded by purple sting rays that turned the water magenta as they twisted through the waves. Purple is my favorite color. It was the most beautiful thing I'd ever seen."

James lowered his voice to a whisper. His smile morphed into a painful stare.

"How did you die?" he asked.

"Like the car that hit you, cancer attacked my pancreas just as fast. I didn't have much time and died a few months after my diagnosis. The doctors did all they could and gave me drugs with funny names and more pills than I could count. Some of the medication made me sicker, and I needed additional drugs to treat the symptoms. Isn't it funny how that happens? In the end, nothing stopped the disease from spreading to the rest of my body. Your father sat by my bedside every day and night. He was with me until the end."

His dad had joined the picnic from the river and

was carrying his fishing pole and tackle box.

"When your mother died, my heart broke again. I didn't think I could go on but somehow found the courage. I was comforted knowing that you'd be here to greet her."

James looked up at his dad with guilt in his eyes.

"But I wasn't there to cross mom over. I was with Victor when she died."

"We know," his mother said. "God told me. I was hoping to see you, but He said I'd have to wait a bit longer because you were doing something special. I'm not mad. I'm proud of the choice you made."

"Want a sandwich, buddy?" Will asked.

His brother offered a half-eaten turkey and cheese in his left hand and playfully punched James's shoulder with his right.

"I missed you, man. Are you going to talk to them the entire time and ignore me?"

James's regret melted away.

"God showed me a vision of your new family at a barbeque. How in the world did you convince anyone to marry you?"

Will leaned in and covered the side of his mouth so his wife wouldn't hear.

"The truth is I tricked her! Thank goodness for my handsome looks and boyish charm. Let me introduce you to Grace."

A thin, elegant woman with dancer's legs rose from the picnic blanket. She reminded James of Lily: dark hair; light-greenish eyes; fair skin. Grace kissed James on his cheek, and he blushed.

"It's so good to finally meet you," she said. "Will talks about you all of the time."

"The pleasure is all mine," James said. "You're

very beautiful."

"That's sweet of you. Welcome home."

"If it wasn't for Grace..." Will slid his arm around his wife. "Well... let's just say that I felt lost for a long time after you died. When she came along, everything fell into place. She even took care of mom when she was sick. Grace is a doctor, and a good one at that."

"That's amazing. Lily wanted to be a nurse. She was kind and compassionate like you."

Grace smiled and rubbed James shoulder.

"And you had a son?" he asked.

"We did, and guess what?" His brother's eyes filled with excitement. "We named him after you. Your nephew is now 40 years old and followed in his mother's footsteps. He's a doctor too and a father of twin girls. Let me tell you, my granddaughters are giving him a run for his money!"

James bit his lower lip.

"You named him after me?"

"Of course — you're my brother, and I love you."

The two embraced, and James accidentally knocked the sandwich out of Will's hand.

"You're still as clumsy as ever. I guess even death can't change some things."

"Maybe I didn't do that by accident."

"Enough," Grandpa interrupted. "You two can fool around later, but right now, it's time to eat!"

They all sat down on the polka-dot blanket and ate as a complete family for the first time in decades. Three generations together at last. They swapped stories of times past, but mostly they laughed as they'd always done. The sky turned auburn as the sun fell below the hills.

"That might be the most beautiful sunset I've seen in heaven," Grandpa said.

James was mesmerized by the kaleidoscope of colors.

"Does it look like this every night?" he asked.

"He's welcoming you home," his father said.

"When I was a spirit guide, I looked up at the sky every night and wondered if God was staring back. I felt a celestial presence but often doubted my intuition and got discouraged."

"God is always speaking to us through nature," his father said. "Pay attention to the omens because they guide us forward."

A loud splash diverted their attention to the river, where a wooden boat glided atop the water. The rickety vessel cut upstream against the current and positioned itself parallel to the meadow. James recognized the oar-less boat from his first trip to paradise. Two tall figures standing shoulder to shoulder were at the bow.

Like the last time, the blond-haired archangel wore a cobalt-colored tunic. His arms were crossed, and his face was stoic. The brown-haired archangel had a similar tunic but it was emerald green. Bright, white light trailed their giant bodies as they walked off the boat and onto the banks of the river. Their feet scrunched the grass. James cranked his neck to get a better look at their expressionless faces.

"How are you, my friends?" Grandpa asked.

The giant wearing the bluish-purple tunic nodded impassively. His companion cloaked in green gave a warm smile and opened his hands in a welcoming gesture.

"Hello," he bellowed in a deep voice that rumbled

the ground and frightened the birds from their perches on the birch tree. They took flight away from the archangels. James felt the vibrations in his feet.

"It's a pleasure to see you again," Raphael said.

"And you as well," Grandpa replied.

The archangel spread his wing-like arms and enveloped the St. George's in emerald light. The floating green particles buzzed around their bodies, melting away any lingering doubt, guilt or pain. The healing effervescence filled them with love. Raphael lowered his arms and the glowing green light disappeared into the birch tree.

"Would you be so kind to return with us to the beach?" the angel asked James, who shot his parents a concerned look. He didn't want to leave them again.

"I promise you won't lose us in heaven," his father explained. "Your journey is almost complete, and you have to go a bit further for it all to make sense."

"We love you so much," his mother added.

"I love you too."

He kissed and hugged them goodbye. Raphael put out his mammoth hand for James to grab. His tiny fingers disappeared in the angel's grasp. Book-ended by the beings of light, James climbed onboard the boat. He recognized the carving of the dragon slayer on the floorboards. The vessel lifted above the water, rotated mid-air and floated downstream before shooting through a tunnel of blinding, white light. This time, he felt anticipation instead of fear.

It was time to meet his maker — again.

CHAPTER 22
THE GOLDEN LIBRARY

The boat shot through the portal at lightning speed. James shielded his eyes from the blinding burst of white and tried to maintain his balance without falling overboard — although it was unclear what falling overboard meant in heaven. He grabbed onto Raphael's arm, which felt like a tree trunk. He concentrated on the muscles in his neck, and ever so slowly forced his head upward to catch a glimpse of the celestial being. The velocity blurred the archangel's face, and James could only make out a fuzzy shape. Raphael appeared unfazed by the dizzying motion, and unlike James, wasn't rocking back and forth.

Without warning, the spinning through space came to an abrupt stop, and the tunnel of light gave way to a cluster of ocean waves breaking against a powdery beach. The rickety boat careened along the calm water and drifted toward the dunes. James marveled at how the heap of weathered wood and rusted nails held together during the violent journey. Then again, much of what'd seen in heaven made little sense.

The pink sand and multi-colored seashells brought back memories of his first trip. The menagerie of aquatic life was the same. He spotted Henry resting on the hot sand. The sea turtle bent his elongated neck and watched James and the archangels float by. He could've sworn the ancient reptile smiled before retreating into his shell. A humpback whale leapt into the horizon and hung midair before gravity pulled the leviathan back into the sea. The subsequent ripple of waves nearly toppled the boat. Purple string rays hovered along the sea floor and illuminated an underwater jungle, including a colony of coral. The creatures swam in a group, and their flat bodies undulated across the sand. Like the sea turtle, the sting rays glanced at the boat.

"He's waiting for you," Raphael said and pointed at two wooden beach chairs on either side of a glass table holding a pitcher filled with sweet tea. Henry stood up from his spot on the sand and started a sluggish trek toward the spot.

"If we move fast enough, then maybe we can beat him," James said. Neither of the archangels smiled at the quip. He rolled his eyes at his humorless bodyguards.

The boat slid onto a sandbar in the surf. James inhaled the ocean air and tasted sea salt. He turned to face the archangels, who reminded him of trees with faces.

"Thank you for bringing me back here."

The heavenly beings nodded but otherwise remained stoic. Their colorful tunics fluttered in the wind. James hopped out of the boat and splashed into the sea. A school of tropical fish swam around him, and like the wildflowers in the meadow, each was more vibrant than the next. The underwater rainbow moved with him as he cut through the waves. Their scaly skin brushed against his legs. Wet sand pushed between his toes. He looked down and realized he was barefoot. His clothes were different too: white-linen pants and a matching button-down shirt. He figured his apparel had changed when he passed through the tunnel. James looked back at his loquacious travel companions, but they were gone, and there was no trace of the boat on the horizon.

"Until next time."

Henry hadn't progressed much in his march across the beach, but he continued parading forward. The contour of his intricate shell was made of vibrant mosaics: yellows and reds mixed with jungle greens and browns. James brushed his fingers along the ancient turtle's rough surface just as he'd scratch a dog's head.

"Do you remember me? I was here a long time ago."

When James reached the chairs, he picked up the pitcher and filled the two glasses with tea. He was thirsty but waited for his host before savoring the cold drink — it would be rude to start without God. He sank comfortably into the chair, closed his eyes and listed to the soothing sounds. The wind whipped around his head and blew grains of sand into his cheeks. A flock of seagulls squawked overhead and a school of dolphins whistled in the water.

Unlike his last visit to the beach, he knew what to expect. Still, he was uncertain how he'd be greeted by God. A flurry of negative thoughts muddled his mind. He looked over at Henry.

"There's nothing I can do about the past, so I might as well enjoy the present."

His eyelids felt heavy. The journey through the portal had sapped his energy. James's shoulders dropped, his arms fell limp and he drifted into a deep slumber that could've lasted for years.

Peaceful.... uninterrupted... long-overdue... sleep.

*

"Beautiful, isn't it?"

James was awoken by a familiar voice, but it wasn't God's.

"I'll never get tired of the vista," the man said. "It's important to center ourselves in nature."

James twisted his head, but the blinding sun obscured his line of sight. He blocked out the glowing orb with his hand and squinted at the stranger's face. As his eyes adjusted and the man's smile came into focus, James nearly fell out of his chair. He knocked over his glass and spilled sweet tea onto his bare feet. Ice cubes slid down his legs.

"Why would you waste such amazing sweet tea — you know it's my favorite."

The man's trimmed gray hair was parted to the side, and his eyes were as blue as the summer sky. His mocha skin wrinkled across his brow and on either ends of his worn lips. The cane was gone, and Jose's back was as straight as an arrow. No more hunch. Like James, he too wore white-linen clothes.

"Is that you?"

"I've been waiting for you," the orderly said. "I told you we'd meet again."

"But I don't understand. Why are you here?"

Jose smiled in a grandfatherly way.

"If you ask too many questions all at once, you'll give yourself a headache, and there's no reason to do that on such a beautiful day."

"I didn't expect you to be here," James said. "I've been waiting for God."

Jose settled into his beach chair. The degenerated discs that once forced his spine to curve were gone, and so was the pain. He grabbed the icy glass and sipped the sweet tea.

"Sometimes, the things we seek appear in ways we don't expect."

James stared incredulously at the old man, who chugged his drink.

"My camouflage allows me to take any form I desire. Sometimes I'm a beggar or a young child or an orderly at a prison."

James's eyes widened to twice their normal size. He squeezed the sides of his chair so hard that his knuckles turned white.

"Why didn't you tell me when we were together? I'd asked for your help! I needed you! I was alone and on my own!"

"The last time we were on this beach, I promised I'd be there to help," God said. "I kept my promise — it's not my fault you were looking for me in the wrong places."

James downed his tea like a shot of whisky; in some ways, he wished it were alcohol.

"If only I'd known, then maybe things would have turned out differently," he said.

God scooped up a handful of sand and let the granules sift through his fingers.

James thought about all the times he'd gazed at the stars hanging high above the prison walls and wondered if God was staring back, not realizing God was standing next to him looking up.

"If I'd revealed myself to you, your true potential would've never been reached. You had to believe you were capable of protecting Victor on your own. Remember, you had lessons to learn."

"I thought Victor was going to die in prison."

"He almost did," God said, laughing loudly. "His peanut allergy nearly killed him. It was a dirty trick by his enemies. I kept him alive in the infirmary."

The sea turtle finally reached the pair and looked up at God with admiration.

"Henry has been with me for longer than I can count," God said. "Sometimes our journeys are more extensive than we anticipated, but if we persist, we'll reach our destination. You should know that better than anyone."

Gazing into God's eyes was like staring into prisms of refracted light. Flashes of colors pulsated within his icy blue iris.

"I'm proud of you," He said. "You did everything I asked of you, and then some. You learned to be courageous, compassionate, loyal, forgiving and loving."

"Loving?"

"Of course! You learned to love your enemy. If only all of my creations could learn that lesson, the world would be a more harmonious place. You protected Victor because your heart was filled with love."

James looked away in disappointment.

"I failed you because I failed Victor. I didn't

protect him like I'd promised. I got distracted and wasn't paying attention to the taxi."

God put his hand on James's arm.

"Like you, Victor had lessons to learn. After taking your life, he needed to show that he valued life beyond his own. Sacrifice was Victor's life lesson."

"I don't understand how I got so distracted. The candles in the church. The owl. Lily."

God poured himself another glass of tea and curled a mischievous smile.

"My creations are everywhere and that includes your friend the owl."

James shook his head with playful disgust and turned his attention to the dolphins bobbing through the water.

"You know, I miss him," James admitted. "Victor was my friend. Funny how that happened — never in a million years did I think I'd befriend the man who killed me."

James brushed aside his hair in the ocean breeze and sank deeper into his chair, wondering whether he'd ever see his buddy again.

"Let's walk to the water," God said. "I have something special to show you."

Together, they sauntered toward an old-wooden pier that jutted into the ocean as far as the eye could see. Henry followed them but lagged behind. They walked down a pink dune and into waves that rippled over a myriad of shells scattering the shoreline. James's feet tingled in the heavenly sea.

"Come take a look," God said.

An underwater swirl scared away the fish. The maelstrom moved faster with each rotation. Its core was a dark and gray. James peered into the eye of the whirlpool, but instead of a family barbeque like he'd seen the last time, he watched a younger, happier Victor pounding away on a typewriter. The keys smacked the white paper, creating an overture of words. His fingers moved at lightning speed. The machine dinged to warn him of the end of the margin. He hit the lever, pushed the barrel and continued composing. The clicking echoed in a grand room filled with mahogany bookcases that lined the walls and stretched from the tiled floor to a cathedral ceiling, but not all of the books were on shelves. Many were stacked to form columns that climbed 20 feet tall.

Victor sat in a crushed, red-velvet armchair and cozied next to a brick fireplace that was so big, a person could comfortably stand in it. Two roaring lions frozen in stone bookended the hearth. A blazing fire provided some light, but the cavernous space glowed mostly from thousands of candles scattered across the library. Each flickering flame danced to the clicks and clacks of the typewriter.

"He's almost finished with the final draft," God said. "I'm sure you'll get the chance to read it."

"I have a feeling I already know what it's about," James said.

"He's making up for lost time. Victor's heaven is filled with books and words. He won't find any damaged texts here. He's at peace."

God turned to James, and the swirl in the water disappeared.

"There's something else I'd like you to see."

CHAPTER 23
ANGELS IN THE WATER

James smelled her perfume before he saw her — a sweet rose scent with hints of amber and a whiff of sandalwood. Lily was leaning against the railing of the pier. She brushed aside wavy strands of blond hair to reveal dimples on both cheeks, complementing an earnest smile. Her blue eyes glowed with radiance. A star pendant dangled from her neck. She moved like a school girl in love. The wind carried her mellifluous voice and tickled his ears.

"I love you."

His lips curled, and his heart swelled with pure bliss. Goosebumps rippled from his shoulders down to his hands. The car crash, the old stone bridge, paradise and the archangels faded into the recess of his mind. The missing puzzle piece was standing before him. Without saying a word, James bolted from the sea and darted past God and Henry. Sharp seashells and scalding-hot sand didn't slow him down. The warped wooden planks rumbled as he sprinted across the pier.

James hoisted Lily into the air, and they locked lips in an everlasting kiss. She brushed her delicate fingers through his. Two souls separated by tragedy had finally become one.

"I've missed you so much," she said softly while gazing into his eyes. "What took you so long?"

"I had to take care of a few things for a guy."

She squished her nose and mouth together in a pout but could only hold the expression for a few seconds before breaking into grin.

"You were always a terrible actor," he said.

Lily playfully slapped his cheek before kissing him again.

"It's been lonely without you." James shook his head with regret. "I never stopped thinking about you since the day I died."

If only he'd known then what he knew now, he would've done a better job of making the best of his time with Lily. She grabbed his hand and pressed it to her cheek.

"My heart's always been with you," she said. "I've never left your side."

A radiating light interrupted their reunion and encompassed their linked bodies in a warm bubble, similar to Raphael's green effervescence that surrounded James's family in the meadow. The couple felt as though they were floating over the sea even though their feet were planted on the pier.

"Where is it coming from?" he asked.

"The light is coming from you," God answered. "Your love is filling this space."

God altered his appearance yet again and resorted back to the form He'd assumed during James's first visit to heaven. The creator morphed into a lanky, bald, muscular, dark-skinned man, but his eyes remained the same — deep-sea blue.

The white glow emanating from James broke into incandescent orbs that clustered above his shoulders. The radiant balls floated like dancing fireflies. When he twisted his torso, the orbs moved with him.

"They're following your every move," Lily said and pointed to his back.

God affectionately grabbed James's arm and pulled him close.

"Congratulations — you're an angel."

"Angel?" James and Lily said simultaneously.

"I promised I'd reward you for undertaking a most difficult task. Not only did I ask you to be a spirit guide but also to protect and shepherd a person who caused you tremendous harm. You persisted through adversity and followed through on your promise. Now, it's time for me to follow through on mine."

"But I never expected to…"

Lily put the tips of her fingers to James's lips, sealed them shut and kissed the ends of her fingertips resting atop his mouth.

"Angels engender peace," God continued. "They're pure, unadulterated beings of light who've never experienced life on earth. On rare occasions, I make exceptions and call upon worthy souls, who exemplify love, courage and faith, to join my service. No one is worthier than you."

James was dumbfounded. He'd never imagined that God would grant him such an honor. Instead, he'd been expecting a rebuke for Victor's unexpected death.

"Why does the light follow me?"

"It's your wings," God replied.

"Like a bird's wings?"

"That's a common misconception perpetuated by storytellers and artists over generations. Ancient myth describes angels as flying beings who live in the clouds. When they first appeared to humans thousands of years ago, angels were mistaken for having feathery wings. In the haze and excitement of interacting with a holy messenger, people misinterpreted the light as instruments of flight, and the image forever stuck."

The glowing orbs hovering above James doubled in size. He reached out to touch the floating balls and was jolted with enlightenment, and his body was infused with a supreme knowledge bestowed upon him by God. Heaven was no longer a physical place but a state of happiness filled with ineffable joy.

"In thy light, you shall see light," God said. "Soon, you'll learn how to control your energy, but for now, admire the beauty."

The orbs lessoned in intensity and shrank to mere flickers.

"Do you like my heaven?" Lily asked.

"Your heaven?"

Lily grabbed James's hands.

"I created it in my dreams — the sweet tea, beach chairs and dolphins. After you died, I cried every night and prayed to God for strength. In the few hours, I managed to sleep, I invented this heaven for you and dreamt you'd meet God on the same beach where we're standing. I fantasized it'd be the place where we'd meet again and watch the sunset together. Every time you looked to the sky for comfort, you saw a glimpse of my heaven."

James brushed aside Lily's hair and kissed her porcelain forehead. Day changed to night as the sun disappeared into the horizon and gave way to the moon and a blanket of stars. The lovers embraced in the milky twilight.

"Fate brought you back together as I'd promised it would," God said. "But before I leave, there's one more thing I'd like to show you."

He gestured toward the end of the pier.

"James, will you walk with me a bit?"

He stared longingly at Lily and didn't want to leave her, but she urged him to go.

"I'll be right here with Henry, so don't worry about me. He'll be my bodyguard."

He kissed her again.

"I promise I'll come right back. I won't be gone for long."

"I love you," Lily said.

"I love you too."

James followed God down the pier, which stretched across the sea. The waves crashed against the pylons supporting the wooden walkway that hovered only a few feet above the water. The splintering boards felt rough on James's toes. A pelican perched on the railing watched the two stroll together in silence. James looked back at Lily, who was standing on the beach. He missed her already.

"Don't worry — you'll see her soon," God said. "You should know by now that I always keep my word."

A school of curious dolphins poked their heads out of the water. James leaned over the railing to get a closer look but lost his balance and nearly fell down.

"I'm sorry," he said. His face flashed three shades

of red. "I don't know what happened. I guess it was wet and I slipped."

But he soon realized that his clumsiness wasn't to blame. The warped boards he was standing on were transforming into blocks of uneven cobblestone. He hoisted himself up and grabbed the railing for support, but it too had changed to stone. The pylons covered in barnacles and seaweed gave way to concrete archways. The ocean churned all around them. James feared he might fall over and into the water.

"What's happening?" he yelled over the explosive noise.

God ignored his cries and stuck out both of his arms to maintain balance. He lifted his lanky legs like a dancer and tiptoed along the changing pier. James crouched down and covered his face from the misty salt water shooting into the air. His stomach churned as the jolting grew more severe.

Then it all stopped.

"What... happened?" he asked wearily.

James felt dizzy, and the world around him was spinning fast. He stood up, pressed one hand to the wall for support and blinked hard at where he was standing.

"I always found the old stone bridge to be a beautiful structure," God said.

James admired the stone crossing in a way he hadn't before. Its simple shape, grayish hue and mixed texture were traits washed out all those years ago by the blinding headlights from Victor's sports coupe.

"The white light you saw that night wasn't from a car," God said. "That was Charlie's light. He was surrounding you with love moments before your death. We're never alone, including the moments before our lives end. Love is always with us."

"But all this time, I thought…"

"Before we talk any further, I want you to look into the water one more time."

The two walked to the south side of the bridge and peered over the stone slate. The river had morphed from an aqua blue to a darker shade. The purple stingrays, colorful fish and ocean bottom filled with coral had disappeared. In its place were millions of people going about their daily lives. A jogger exercised in a park. A firefighter steered a ladder truck down a narrow street. A mother pushed an infant in a stroller. A doctor scrubbed in for surgery. A teacher lectured to a classroom filled with students. A family ate dinner around a kitchen table. The world was alive with energy, and next to each and every person was a white glow in the shape of a sphere. The orbs followed the people wherever they went.

"What are the balls of light?" James asked.

"They're guardian angels busy at work."

"There are so many of them"

"Indeed, there are. There's a lot to do. Angels are everywhere, helping and protecting."

"What's happening there?"

James pointed to hundreds of shining orbs that had fallen into a vast body of water, disappearing underneath the surface.

God shook his head with sadness.

"A terrible thing I'm afraid — a plane crash."

Within seconds, hundreds of orbs reappeared and broke through the water's surface, but this time, they were twice as bright and three times as large. The orbs climbed high and passed through the clouds.

"The angels are crossing souls to the other side and bringing them here," God said. "Soon, they'll be with you and me."

The light in the river around James and God got brighter. The vignettes of the world disappeared, and the old stone bridge was engulfed in a warm glow. The orbs exploded out of the water and shot mist in different directions. James shielded his face from the mini-blasts. He tried to count them, but there were too many. Each ball of light had a human face: a man; a woman; a child. Their eyes were closed. They looked peaceful as they passed James and God and climbed high into the sky, where they disappeared among the stars.

"Where will they go?"

"They're headed to their own heavens. I'll greet each one as I did you."

"Are all angels guardian angels?"

"No," God answered. "There are different types of angels for different tasks. Some guide souls. Others deliver messages, while some have the power to heal and perform miracles. They're extensions of me in one form or another."

God smiled at James.

"There are still adventures for you — the learning never ends."

James smiled back and together they walked across the cobblestones to the other side of the bridge.

ABOUT THE AUTHOR

Matt Kozar is a former Emmy-award winning journalist, who worked at WCBS-TV and WABC-TV in New York City. He received a bachelor's degree in economics from Brown University and a master's degree in journalism from Columbia University. Following the death of his brother, Doug, he's written extensively about drunk driving.

Made in the USA
Columbia, SC
24 May 2018